Other Books by Tony Jordan

The Train
Flying Blind
Follow Me and Other Stories
Breakfast with Faulkner
Spies, Assassins, and Such

All are available online at Amazon, Barnes and Noble,
Books-a-Million, and Kindle.

— A —
CHRISTMAS CAROL
FOR GROWN-UPS

and other stories by
TONY JORDAN

SPY HILL
PUBLISHING

Spy Hill Publishing

First Edition

Library of Congress Control Number: 2017954191
Spy Hill Publishing, Clinton, TN

ISBN-13: 9780692937143
ISBN-10: 0692937145

Book and cover design by Nathan Armistead
Printed in the United States of America

For my father,
for whom Christmas was the best time of the year,
and for my son Andrew,
who missed Christmas by a week.
We miss them both, but will continue to celebrate the season
in their memory.

CONTENTS

— A —
Christmas Carol
for Grown-Ups

A Christmas Carol for Grown-Ups

It was the best season of the year.

"Christmas time is here..." sang John Pizzarelli. It was a straight-up Vince Guaraldi arrangement, with the pianist and bass backing John's guitar. Amazing how like Diana Krall John's voice sounded—a throaty alto, not quite so mellow as Mel Torme's would have been, but then, Mel Torme was no longer with us.

"Snowflakes in the air..." And there were. The weatherman was calling for an accumulation of three to four inches before morning. Not enough to cause trouble getting around the city, but certainly enough to give an appearance of noonday to objects below—after the clouds blew out, of course.

Last month he had enjoyed the Macy's parade, and later, visits to the Met and to FAO Schwarz. This was for him, as it was for the children in the song, his favorite time of year. Tonight he was enjoying an early dinner at the Café Carlyle while listening to a classic jazz performer who never disappointed.

His companion was lively. They talked of Christmas seasons past, of people in the publishing business, of politicians. She occasionally leaned over to pat his hand or so that he could share a confidence with her. They laughed, but mostly they listened to John's performance.

Tomorrow night they had tickets to the New York City Ballet production of *The Nutcracker.* He never missed a year of the Christmas ballet, and he made it a point to queue up every third year or so to see the Rockettes at Radio City Music Hall. It really wasn't the Rockettes he went to see. It was just being in the music hall that he liked so much. Of course, the electronic instruments played by the small orchestra fascinated him. The bright-blue neon-wrapped bass and the futuristic electric violins. They reached something of the child in him.

He had tried adding the Philharmonic's *Messiah* to his holiday routine but found it tiresome. The famed "Hallelujah" chorus was difficult to botch, but the rest of the lengthy performance depended way too much on the particular singers who were performing that year, and too often there was only a single great. The other one and two—or even three—main soloists might be so-so, and there was little to do but suffer through their solos. Moderate talent could not perform the *Messiah.* After two tries in three years, he struck it from his New York City Christmas list. Now he looked for smaller venues offering selected Christmas music.

Sometimes the choirs he chose sang the "Hallelujah" chorus, and he could enjoy just that without having to endure a contralto reaching beyond her range for notes or a basso profundo unable to achieve the vibrato of an exceptionally low note. On the whole, he found the church choirs' Christmas concerts to be more enjoyable than the New York Philharmonic's *Messiah*.

And then there was John Pizzarelli and his band. One received consistently professional performances from that group, and when John's wife, Jessica Molaskey, had joined the trio— well, it's what you went to New York for. That, and the various "jazz manouche" and "swing jazz" some of the hotel bars and clubs could provide. He followed two of these groups closely and made sure he could take in at least one performance of each during his visits to the city. Carte Blanche seemed to be getting more gigs than Avalon Jazz Band these days—which was too bad, for he thought Tatiana Eva-Marie was a much more animated singer than the young ladies who sang with Carte Blanche. Oh well, tonight was about the consistent high quality that pros like Pizzarelli and Molaskey offered. They never disappointed.

At the end of John's performance, after the applause had died away, he and his companion rose to leave. A woman at a table farther out from the stage asked her husband, "Isn't that Hope Merriweather?"

Her husband strained to look without appearing to look. "Ahhh...where?"

"Up near the stage."

"Oh yes, I think you're right. If it isn't, she's a double." He used the opportunity of his wife looking away to steal another bite of her remaining double-dark chocolate mousse.

"Well, who's that she's with?"

Caught with the mousse in his mouth, he mumbled, "I have no idea. Never seen him before." That's what he meant, but to her it sounded like, "Eee-ha-no-eye-dee. Nev-see-hee-for."

A woman at the next table, having overheard the conversation, leaned across. "I think that's Jack Blaine. I read something in one of the gossip pieces in the *Times* or the *Post* about Hope Merriweather being seen out with a 'mystery man.' The reporter was pretty sure it was Blaine."

"Who's Jack Blaine?" the first lady asked.

"Not really sure, other than he obviously has money. You don't see very much about him, but there are all kinds of stories—like he's the bastard son of you-know-who and inherited all his money. Or there's the one that he's really the brains behind two or three Wall Street firms. But the story people seem to like most is that he found a buried treasure and has been selling off the pieces bit by bit for years."

The first lady had no idea of who "you-know-who" was, but she was intrigued that the head of one of the largest publishing firms in New York would be out in public with a mystery man. Looking at her husband, his mouth full of mousse, and then back at the man holding Merriweather's chair, she could only sigh. The man across the room was six feet or perhaps just under, his steel-gray hair full and nicely groomed. His face was tanned, setting off all the more his closely trimmed cavalry moustache, chin patch, and beard. He wore not a tux but a black velvet jacket with tuxedo trousers. The trousers had a West Point cut and fit perfectly over the tops of his black boots, the heels of which, to a practiced eye, carried spur ridges.

The outfit was cut perfectly and fit him like the uniform of a gentleman. His tie was a wide, nineteenth-century bow tie, which drooped down the front of his shirt, giving him the look of a writer of some import. It was a good look for him, and you could tell from the way he moved that he was in good shape. He had a diagonal scar on the right side of his face that, on another man, would have been a disfigurement, but on him seemed simply to indicate that he might be a dangerous man.

The lady sighed a second time, but then remembered just how much money her husband made in a year and turned contentedly back, taking her napkin and wiping the mousse from the edges of his mouth.

The woman across from her heard the sigh and agreed that Jack Blaine, if that was him, was not a bad-looking man.

The not-bad-looking man pulled the chair out for his companion who, indeed, was Hope Merriweather, and after retrieving Ms. Merriweather's coat, strolled with her out of the café and into the lobby of the Carlyle Hotel. Outside, he saw her into a cab. He gave the driver her address, which was a bit farther up the East Side on the Park. Returning to the café bar, he ordered a cognac, which he sipped for perhaps ten minutes before he retrieved his coat, hat, and cane from the checkroom and left the hotel through a side door. He walked around the corner to another cabstand and gave the driver an address a little farther up the East Side on the Park. Arriving at the address, he used a swipe card to enter the underground parking garage and then to take the elevator to the top floor, bypassing the doorman. Even in 2013, the proprieties must be observed.

The rest of the evening and the weekend passed in a most pleasant fashion. Were this an adventure story, the narrator would be explicit in the pleasantries of the sex. Were it a romantic novel, the sex would be more implied, but the pleasure would be the same. Even if it is simply a story for grown-ups, suffice it to say both parties arose Monday morning eager to tackle the week. Ms. Merriweather was off to her office, and Mr. Blaine, if indeed that was who he was, returned to his hotel, packed his case, and headed for Penn Station. He took a midmorning train to Washington, DC, where he checked in to a small but elegant executive hotel in Alexandria, Virginia.

"A pleasure to see you again, Mr. Le Roi," the silver-haired desk clerk said.

"A pleasure to see you again, Roger," the gentleman replied.

"Per your request, you're in the Robert E. Lee Suite. We've held, I believe it is twelve, messages for you," he said, handing over the pink slips on which the messages were written.

"Thank you, Roger." He took the slips and, stuffing them in his overcoat pocket, picked up his bag. As he did, a bellman dove for the handle of the leather duffel but pulled up quickly when he caught Roger's look of admonition.

Taking his bag, Mr. Le Roi disappeared up the steps to his right and down the connected hallway as the bellman bent himself around the corner to watch him depart.

"He always carries his own bag," Roger explained.

"Really?" was all the bellman could muster in reply.

"Been coming here for years. Started before I was employed, and that's been twenty years next spring. By the way, if anyone asks you anything about him, you know nothing. Understand?"

"Yeah well, I *don't* know anything. Who is the guy?"

"All you need to know is that he is a very valued client of this hotel who continues to patronize us because we are discreet. Failure to be so will cost you your job and us a very good client."

"Did I hear you call him Lee Roy? The bellman emphasized the "Lee," and a look that threatened murder—or at least severe bodily harm—fell across the manager's face.

"No, you did *not* hear me say, 'Lee Roy.' I said, 'Le Roi.' It's French, and you'd best learn to pronounce it correctly. Didn't they teach you about correct pronunciation of names at the Ritz?"

"Yeah—sure they did. I just never ran up against many French people, that's all."

"Well, Mr. Le Roi isn't French. Well, not that I know of. I mean, his forwarding address is in Tennessee. I think Frank up in the restaurant may know more about him. He always asks for Frank to wait his table."

Upstairs, Mr. Le Roi unpacked his bag, changing into a pair of Levi's jeans, a flannel shirt, and a pair of somewhat beat-up looking, but very expensive, Roper boots. He took a maroon wool baseball jacket from his bag, along with a maroon baseball cap that had a large, gold *L* on it and, leaving his room, walked from the hotel to the nearest metro stop. He caught a Yellow Line train into the District, changing to the Red Line and then exiting at McPherson Square. He walked to the church and entered through the back basement door.

"Good evening!" he said to no one in particular. Still, most looked up. Some smiled, while others just returned to what they were doing. "Good evening, Thaddeus!" This to the priest who was wearing an apron and struggling to move a large pot of what smelled like stew from a stove.

"Good evening," the priest responded. "Little help here, please."

Almost bouncing the two steps forward, Le Roi grabbed up two potholders and caught onto the handles of the pot just in time to keep its contents from transforming from stew into floor cleaner.

Placing the pot on the stainless-steel counter, the priest turned. "And how was your trip?"

"Very nice. Hope says hello."

"And hello to Hope. I thought you said you'd try to get her to come down."

"And try I did, classmate of mine. But she remains very resistant to our overtures. She isn't one to be trifled with, and she still hasn't forgiven you for taking the cloth."

"J.B., she was never in love with me. You know that. She always had a thing for you."

"True as that may be, my friend, you know her feelings about 'the brotherhood,' as she refers to it."

"But that was more than forty years ago. My God, we're in our sixties. How on earth can she still be mad?" The priest stirred the stew with a gigantic spoon.

"I don't think she's angry. I think she very much wants to see you, but you know how hardheaded she's always been. She thinks you betrayed those of us who are freethinkers. And don't convoke God into the discussion. You should say three Hail Marys." He reached up, taking an apron from its peg and replacing it with his baseball jacket. Putting the apron over his head, he tied the strings behind his back.

"Well, this has got to stop." The priest frowned. "I didn't betray anybody. I thought this was the best way to help people. Besides, if she's so against the brotherhood, what does she think about what *you* do? I mean, what is it you told me they call you at the Agency? The 'warrior priest,' was it? You might as well have taken holy orders. You're a priest as much as I am. Look at what you do these days."

Walking over, Le Roi placed his finger on the lips of his friend.

"Enough. I told you that in the confidence of the confessional. You know enough of my philosophy to know that I could never truly be a priest, and Hope does not know what I do...rather, what I did. And she'll never learn from you. Are we agreed?"

Looking only a little sheepish, the smaller man agreed.

"And besides, she's coming down Friday afternoon. I've made a reservation for her at the Hay-Adams."

The priest grinned and raised the spoon as if to strike his friend.

"I should use this spoon as the jawbone of an ass and smite you as a Philistine. Lead me into temptation, will you!"

"Temptation, is it? I thought you found no interest in the fairer sex. Your words betray you, Father. And, of course, that is the greatest of the legion of reasons I could not be a priest—and one for which I am in no way sorry."

"No, my son, it is the temptation to do murder that you present. While I admit I see no valid theological reason that priests should not marry, I am not often tempted by women—although I have sometimes wondered how Hope might have perceived me had I not taken holy orders."

"Well, I don't know how she might have looked at you, but I've never seen you as anything but Brother or Father Thaddeus. Even when we were in college, I assumed you would go on to seminary. You were meant for the priesthood even when you tried to convince us—and yourself—there was no God."

"And now here I am, forty-plus years later, doing exactly what I did forty-plus years ago. No richer and alas, no wiser."

"Thaddeus, it's forty-four years ago. Be precise when using numbers, and you literally ooze wisdom from your pores. Say three more Hail Marys for your passive-aggressive effort to seek confirmation." J.B. took a small spoon and tasted the stew.

"Needs salt—and a little black pepper wouldn't hurt."

"Are you sure?" Father Thaddeus was always light on the seasoning, preferring to allow his clients to season their own meals.

"Sure, I'm sure. Have I ever been wrong about cooking?"

Musing for a moment, the priest leaned over, picked up a large saltcellar, and dosed the stew with three hefty shakes, after which he put the spoon back in and stirred the pot again.

Tonight they would serve more than a hundred hungry homeless again. If they were the only place in town offering free meals, that would still be too many homeless people; but they were in fact one of many soup kitchens throughout the city providing this service. The Mitch Snyder Center would serve hundreds and provide beds as well. St. Michael's had no beds, but it could do an evening meal and, in the mornings, offer coffee, tea, and day-old pastries. The coffee was hot, and even two-day-old doughnuts soften up when you dip them in a hot liquid.

So, Jackson Blaine Le Roi, aka Jack Blaine or just J.B., took his place in the serving line ladling stew to the hungry of Washington, DC. After dinner, he would scrub the pots clean before sharing a final cup of coffee with his friend and then returning to his hotel to act upon the messages that awaited him on the pink slips and in his e-mail.

Every afternoon that week, he helped prepare the food, and every evening, he helped to serve and clean up. Every afternoon, that is, except the following Friday, which found him at Union Station.

She came out of the exit, a porter in tow, looking like the successful businesswoman she was. Tallish, thin, aristocratic—she was dressed in a blue wool dress over which she wore a heavy, gray cloak and a curly wool Cossack hat that, with her tall riding boots, only added to the illusion that Catherine the Great was striding through Union Station. You expected to see four or five Russian wolfhounds attending her. The collar of the dress showed through the cloak, setting off her intense blue eyes. Not a single person in the station would have put her age at more than fifty, yet she was sixty-five.

There was no intimacy in the greeting. He simply took her arm and whisked her toward a town car waiting in front of the station. Arriving at the Hay-Adams, he gave the bell captain a suite number for her luggage and escorted her to the accommodation he had reserved for her. When the bellman had delivered the luggage, he tipped him, closed the door, and said, "I don't know if I should say this is really brave of you, that your visit is twenty years overdue, or just that I'm glad you came."

"How about all of them? You know I love Thad like a brother and have stayed away only because I didn't want to hurt him."

"Yes—well—I think your staying away has hurt him more than your not believing in God; but we've had that discussion, and it's over. You're here now, and that's what matters."

"Are you sure he doesn't know you know?" She asked almost sotto voce.

"Yes, I'm absolutely sure. Well…as absolutely sure as you can be when you're dealing with someone who has heard confessions for forty years and knows a lie before it is uttered."

"I know. That's what absolutely petrifies me," she answered. "Thad always knew when I was lying. I could see it in his eyes. He never called me on a single one that I told him, but I knew he knew."

"And it made you not want to lie to him anymore, right?" He helped her off with her cloak. "That's the beauty of Thad's method," he continued. "He doesn't challenge you, but he makes you challenge yourself. Talk about guilt. He can make you feel guilty without even looking at you. I'm convinced he does it telepathically. And when you silently reach the conclusion that you're not going to lie again and will try to do better somehow, he communicates to you that he is pleased, and then you feel pleased. You leave the confessional or conversation feeling better than when you came in. It's a gift that he uses to help others. Sometimes I wonder, though, just what the costs are for him."

"Costs?" she asked as she sat in a chair and indicated she needed help removing a boot by reaching her leg out and kicking him, then shaking the toe of the boot.

"Yes, cost. Think of the sin he's heard about in forty years. I know it's mostly, 'Father, forgive me, for I lusted in my heart,' but I bet there was a lot more to it than that. To truly grant absolution, you must take upon yourself the sins confessed to you and then hand them off to God...but since you don't believe in God, then it's even more of a quandary. If there's no God to hand them off to, what does he do with them?"

"I see. So, you're saying what we've known since we were eighteen? That Thaddeus Cawthorne is a very strong person?"

"Strong, yes. Superman, I don't think so. Imagine encountering people on a daily basis knowing the most evil things they have thought of doing or even might have done. You have to treat them as if you didn't know. Think of the strength that takes. Think of the wear and tear—not just on your mind but also on your soul. Again, since you don't believe in a soul, just consider the mental anguish that knowing everyone else's secrets could cause."

By this time, she had wiggled out of her dress and slip and was pulling some Wrangler jeans up her extremely long and still nicely muscled legs. "But my dear, I'm the very best publisher in New York. I *do* know everyone's secrets. Well, everyone that anyone would want to read about, but…"

Pulling a red cotton sweatshirt over her head, her voice became muffled.

"…But OK, I get it. His life has been a lot tougher than mine, reading manuscripts and manipulating authors. Or yours. Say…what exactly *were* you doing all those years you were traveling around the world?"

"Oh, come on. I've told you a million times. I was a consultant who assessed business climates for clients, and I did due diligence on potential foreign business partners. It's hard to do business in some countries if you don't have the right contacts and know the form. But we're not here to talk about me—or for that matter, you—although you do know I will talk about you at any time."

He stood behind her and ran his hands up under her sweatshirt, caressing her breasts. He remembered the first time he had done so. They had both been twenty, and it had been in his apartment in New Orleans. Then, she had turned in toward him and pulled her shirt over her head. Today, she turned in toward him, kissed him lightly on the lips, and said, "How can you think about sex at a time like this?"

She sat and drew on a pair of leather walking shoes. After tying them up, she gathered her hair into a ponytail, threading it through the back of a one-size-fits-all New York Yankees' ball cap. Standing, she grabbed a fleece jacket from one of her suitcases and announced, "Let's go."

She wasn't sure what to expect, but whatever it was, it wasn't what she got. When they entered the basement room from its outside door, dinner was in full swing. There was a roar of voices. The room was steamy at one end from the kitchen and at the other from body heat. The smell of wet wool and human sweat hung heavy in the moist air. The closer they got to the kitchen, the more the aroma changed from wet dog and body odor to hot stew and heated-up bread. Although most of the table space was already occupied, the line was still long.

A sports whistle abruptly halted the conversation, and Father Thaddeus announced, "People, we have more than a few here tonight, so please don't put your coats and possessions on the benches next to you. Put them on the floor between your legs. I assure you, those who would steal in the house of God—even his basement—would be struck down with one of the ten plagues, so please welcome someone to sit next to you."

Father Thaddeus had leaned out over the serving counter to make the announcement, and now he leaned back to continue slicing bread, the whistle cord around his neck almost falling victim to the knife on the next slice. The bread had been donated by the bakery down the street. Like the dough-nuts served in the mornings, the bread was a day old—but it had been heated in the oven, so it had a crusty outside and a warm inside. Put some margarine on it and you wouldn't know the difference from hot fresh bread.

There was no time for long hellos or, for that matter, hellos of any length. J.B. grabbed aprons from the pegs and, helping Hope from her jacket, put the apron over her head and took her to the return tray area, where those who had finished their meals were returning the trays and detritus of their meals. He showed her how to get the garbage into the right receptacles and the trays into the hot dishwater. He offered her a pair of rubber gloves—which she gladly accepted—and then he ventured out among the tables helping those with children or those with handicaps to clean up their trays and tables. He went to the door to check the line and came back to assess how much more food they might need and whether the servers needed to decrease the portion size to accommodate all those in line.

Friday nights were always heavy, but this evening the crowd seemed even larger than usual. At one point, Thaddeus ran down the block to the bakery, asking if he could have the day-old bread before it was a day old. The bakery provided him with several loaves of the less-favorite varieties of the day, and he took them back to the basement and sliced them thinly.

As they neared closing time, they still had people in line. One of the men, who was not a regular, seemed agitated. As the server ladled the stew onto his tray, he became vocal.

"Fish stew! Goddamned fish stew! I thought the pope told you guys it was OK to eat meat on Fridays. We need meat!" He banged his hand on the counter. "Meat! It's too goddamned cold and wet out there not to have meat. Come on, if you guys are going to offer meals for us, we deserve respect. Meat! Good meat, not stew meat! I'm so goddamned sick of stew. I have it every night. Why can't you make some steak suppliers feel guilty enough to give you steaks, or do you keep that just for the priests and their concubines!"

He railed on another ten or so seconds before J.B. reached him. Taking the lapels of his very dirty coat, J.B. looked him in the eye and very calmly said, "Brother, you don't have to eat it. We're almost out of food, and I'm sure there's someone else in line who would like it, so either take your tray and sit, or leave it for another person."

The man started to respond, but after looking into J.B.'s deep green eyes, he did not. He took his tray and, receiving a piece of bread from Father Thaddeus and some Jell-O salad from the next server, found a place at a table as close to the door as he could get.

Looking out over the now-quiet room, J.B. smiled. "God bless us, every one."

The conversation picked up again, and the line kept moving.

They finished cleaning at eight thirty, and all the volunteers were gone by nine, leaving only Father Thaddeus, J.B., and Hope. J.B. pulled a cell phone from his pocket as he hung up his apron and helped Hope off with hers.

"Charlie, we're ready," was all he said.

He turned to Hope and Thaddeus, who were standing about four feet apart looking at each other, totally befuddled as to the protocol of what happened next.

"Father Thad, Hope. Hope, Father Thad," J.B. said as he gathered Hope with his right arm and Thad with his left—pulling them into what he had imagined would become a three-way hug. It did, but not the hug he had imagined. Instead the embrace felt forced and distant—air kiss, hug; air kiss, hug. Still, keeping them within his arms, J.B. pushed them gently toward the door of the basement, out and up the stairs, and into the waiting town car. Inside, he sat between them and bade the driver, "Home, Charlie."

Home—which was the Robert E. Lee Suite at J.B.'s small and exclusive hotel—was welcoming. The fire in the fireplace was gas, and the room was scented with balsam sprigs and wreaths. Three stockings hung from the mantel with the letters *T*, *H*, and *J* embroidered upon them. The bar was set, along with a table of savories and sweets, including Russian caviar, lox, and dove's eggs. On the sweet side of the table were pecan pie, fruitcake (not the doorstop kind, but the kind full of nuts and candied fruit that even those who publicly adjured fruitcake enjoyed in private), and a dark chocolate flan. The sitting room held a leather sofa in front of the fireplace flanked by two leather club chairs. The hardwood floor was a medium-dark cherry, the paintings (not prints) were portraits and landscapes, the carpets were expensive Oriental, the drapes were heavy and closed. It was very much a room one would expect to find described in a novel about the antebellum South or in an English country house murder mystery.

The music, low and soft and coming from hidden speakers, was not Christmas music, but Madeline Peyroux singing the blues in French.

"My, my!" Hope observed. "I would have expected nothing less from Mr. Christmas."

"*Tres jolie*," Father Thad extolled in his best bayou French.

At the use of the Cajun French expression, Hope cut her eyes toward Thad, raising the corner of her mouth at the same time as if to say, "Attempting to call up forty-year-old memories is unfair." But she said instead, "What was it all the tourists would say on Bourbon Street? '*Laissez les bon temps rouler*'?"

"Yes," J.B. replied, "and you used to roll your eyes toward them the same way you just did toward Thad."

He moved to the bar. "Hope, shall I make you a Sazerac or would you rather I made a pitcher of martinis?"

"No, I think a Sazerac might be called for." She took off her jacket, looking for someplace to put it, but ended up throwing it over the arm of the sofa.

"Thad, a Sazerac or straight Irish for you?"

"Well, I suppose I could have one Sazerac, for old time's sake."

"Then three Sazeracs it is. Remember when we all had our first real Sazeracs? The Blue Room Bar in the Roosevelt

Hotel. God, that was a long time ago." He swirled the absinthe around each of the glasses. "We were eighteen…let's see, that's how many years? My math isn't all that good…let's see, sixty-six minus eighteen—"

"Is more than I care to contemplate," Hope cut in, handing him the bottle of Peychaud's bitters. "And besides, it's sixty-five, not sixty-six. You never could count."

"No, no. You got that all wrong. I know you heard that from people, but they weren't saying I *couldn't* count…they were saying I *was* a no count. You just heard it wrong." He had expected to get at least a groan, or her patented eye roll of dismissal. Failing even that, he said, "I see I have a tough crowd tonight."

He handed her a Sazerac and reached another over the back of the sofa to Thad, who had seated himself in one corner of the long couch. Thad was backed in as if he might need to defend his position. J.B. escorted Hope to the other end of the sofa, indicating she should sit. He then placed himself in the club chair nearest her. He knew she didn't need his protection, but he felt protective all the same.

Raising his glass, J.B. offered, "To us, and those like us." It was a toast he had learned in the military. The standard response was, "Damned few left," but he did not expect either Thad or Hope to have heard it before.

He was surprised when Hope responded, "Damned few left."

She looked at him. "I've published more than a few military memoirs, and I can't tell you how many times I've heard that one."

Thad seemed appropriately impressed, raised his glass, and then sipped the Sazerac, because it was not a drink to be gulped, guzzled, or even from which medium swallows should be taken. It was meant to be sipped. Thad had learned this from the bartender at the Blue Room those many years ago when he had visited the bar a day in advance of a scheduled appointment with his compatriots. He had made it a point to sample both the drink and the venue in advance so that he would look "cool" when the three kept their appointment the next day. And look cool he had. Even J.B. had been impressed. Thad knew what was in the drink and how to make it, and he had insisted on ordering it with the original recipe of cognac instead of the then-trendy bourbon. He had seemed a man of the world to the two friends who had had faced him then and who sat facing him now. Together again, after so many years. Thad seemed not to know how or where to begin. He turned his face toward J.B., who had become a true man of the world.

J.B., taking his glass from his lips but continuing to hold it in both hands and look over the rim, started.

"Well, I don't know any other way to begin this than to jump in with both feet. Here we are assembled once more, *les trois amis*." They had always spoken French because one, they could; two, it had separated them from the other students; and three, it allowed them a certain privacy when making jokes or observations.

"More like one friend and two traitors." Hope's voice carried an undertone of bitterness. "Look at us now. A priest, an old maid, and a spy. Oh yes!" she said, rounding on J.B. "I know all about your charade and your antics as a business consultant.

"In addition to the military memoirs I've published, I also published a few CIA tell-alls—and on more than one occasion, I read the original manuscripts before they were scrubbed by the Agency's Publications Review Board. So, when I read the stories in which some of the authors tell of the redoubtable officer known as the Scout or the Warrior Priest, I started to ask them who he was. True to their oaths, they never told me his name, but some of them described him to me, and—poof!— one day, fifteen years ago, I was waiting for you in the bar in the Carlyle. You came in, stopped, and scanned the room, and I knew. It was something one of the former CIA guys told me about why you were called the Scout. About how you took in every corner before you entered a room. I saw you, and I knew. It was you they had been describing."

J.B. looked shocked. "Fifteen years? You've known for fifteen years, and you've been deceiving me all this time!" He was relieved but still shocked. His attempt at humor did not deter her. She pressed on.

"Why should I believe anything you say any more than Father Thad over there? Father Thad, the 'freethinker!'" She emphasized "Father" and "freethinker" through extremely tight lips. "The freethinker who helped me shed the impediments of my religious youth and realize there was no God. That we are alone in the world, and it's all about survival of the fittest. I go to Europe for graduate school, and next thing I know, he's in seminary praying on his knees to a God he convinced *me* didn't exist!

"And you're just as bad. Reading Sartre and Camus in French and quoting them all the time. Black T-shirts under seersucker coats and Gauloises cigarettes. Do you know how much I hate the smell of Gauloises cigarettes?

"Your 'war isn't the answer' essays in political science. You debating the ROTC guys over the meaning of duty and honor. You even led the 'Elect Humphrey' campaign at both Tulane and Loyola. I mean, you were as antiwar as they come.

"But when I come back from Oxford, you're in the army, and then you go to Vietnam, and I don't hear from you for almost ten years. Then you show up like nothing has changed except you have scars all over your body that you won't tell me the truth about. I don't believe for a minute they're from a helicopter accident.

"You act like nothing has changed, and you want us to be twenty years old again. You come to New York every Thanksgiving, and we have a good time. Sometimes you show up other times and we have dinner, but you're off again to who knows where, giving me some story of a client with a problem. We always go to my apartment, and you never invite me to wherever it is you live full time. For all I know, you might live in New York and you're married and have five kids and I'm just a piece you keep on the side.

"Then I come down here, and one of the first things I hear you say is 'God bless us every one.' What bullshit! I mean, I've read some unmitigated bullshit from a lot of people who thought they could write, but that 'God bless us, every one' is the most arrogant piece of bullshit I've ever heard *anyone* espouse."

She was getting wound pretty tight, so J.B. moved from his chair to the arm of the couch, attempting to put his arm around her. But she was having none of his solicitous behavior.

"No, don't touch me! I don't need you. I've never needed anyone but myself." Looking at Thad—"You taught me that! And now, goddamn it, you're going to make me feel guilty that I've neglected you all these years."

She looked as if she might throw the glass she held. J.B. placed himself between her and Thad.

"Hope, this is all my fault. I guess if we're playing 'tell the truth,' I should come clean. I got you down here under false pretenses. Thad doesn't have cancer."

She stood quickly, snatching up her jacket from the arm of the sofa.

"But I knew you wouldn't come otherwise. You're too proud, and your hurt is too deep."

She was trying to find the arm of her jacket, the tears clouding her eyes. J.B. was trying to keep her from putting it on.

"Actually, J.B., that isn't true." This from Thad.

"What isn't true? That's she's too proud?"

"No, that I don't have cancer."

J.B. and Hope stopped fighting over the jacket. Hope collapsed on the sofa as if her legs had given out. J.B. stood with his jaw slack.

"You have cancer?" An almost simultaneous question from Hope and J.B.

Silence hung over the carefully decorated room, like a mourner waiting for a eulogy to begin. Then Thad spoke.

"Yes, prostate cancer. The doctors don't think it has spread, and they tell me it's slow growing, so we have time to consider options. I wasn't going to tell either of you. Strange how the truth has a way of finding its way out."

Hope sat drying her eyes with a handkerchief J.B. had handed her. J.B. sat down in the chair, his head in his hands. Silence once again hovered in the room like an unwanted phantasm. The only sound was the ticking of the carriage clock on the mantel over the silent gas fire.

Taking rather too large a sip of his Sazerac, Thad coughed as the cognac went down too fast. The cough broke the spell.

Placing his glass on the sofa table over the back of the couch, he observed, "Hope is right. We're not twenty anymore. We're different people. Forty years is too much to overcome. Still, if we can't capture that which we had, is there a chance we might create something new—or are we too different and too old? As for the cancer, I am reliably informed that the success rate for this type of cancer at my age and health is remarkably good, so while I appreciate your concern, depending upon what transpires this weekend, we may or may not discuss this further. You know what I know at the moment, but tonight I think we should talk about us. And right now J.B. seems to want to address that."

J.B. took his head from his hands. He stood, moving toward the fire, for a sudden chill had passed through him and left him feeling his age. His hands on the mantel, he leaned in toward the fire and then turned, placing his hands behind his back.

"No, I won't accept that we're different. Experience only magnifies who we are. We are still the same three eighteen-year-olds who met in college. Remember, 1965? Thad and I were roommates at Loyola, and we ventured out to a fraternity mixer at Tulane, where we discovered this tall, vivacious, gorgeous, redheaded minx from Sophie Newcomb College who was giving better than she got from the fraternity boys. It was chemistry. Her French was from France—or so it seemed—and ours was from the Gulf Coast. She kept correcting us until the third glass of that vile purple concoction they were serving, and then she fell into the same Cajun slang we were using. Her cover was blown. She was from a big house up on Bayou Lafourche, and not New Orleans. That very evening, we became *les trois amis,* and we still are. I simply will not accept that we are different people because I know we're not."

Neither Hope nor Thad said anything. Hope picked up her glass and settled back into her corner of the sofa. Thad did the same.

J.B. started to continue, but Hope interrupted. "No, J.B.— what about all the secrets? We're not the same. We never had secrets from one another when we were in college. We shared everything. Thad was the brother I never had, and you...you were the love of my life. I idolized you. You could do no wrong.

You told me it wouldn't matter if I went to Oxford—that what we had would last. I believed you."

Her glass empty, she stood and edged around to the bar table. Taking a new glass, she briefly considered the choices before pouring it half full of a single malt scotch. "I believed you, and for forty years, I've measured every other man against you, and they've come up wanting." She sat down again, contemplated the scotch in the glass, and then took a considerable swig.

"And for forty years, I have kept coming back to you," J.B. said.

"Hope, if we're telling secrets, then let me share one more. I'm sterile. Have been for thirty-eight years. Never be any little Le Rois running around solving problems. No more math geniuses like my father or sister…and it's the reason why you didn't see me for so long.

"Thad knows some of this," J.B. continued. "Sorry, Thad, but I never really said any of those Hail Marys or Our Fathers you suggested. It's just that when you're in the intelligence business, a priest is much better than a psychiatrist since the latter can get you grounded from fieldwork or even dismissed from the agency. So, I sought you out because I had to tell someone what I was going through…but I didn't tell you everything."

His hands behind his back, he faced out. Chest and chin up, he looked like he was a commanding officer delivering a brief to his troops, or perhaps just a politician preparing to offer another palliative thought to his constituency.

"In December of 1971, while I was still in the army, I was working for an interservice group that was searching for POW camps in Northern Laos and North Vietnam. The CIA had some local agents they had recruited who were passing on information they picked up in towns and villages in the regions. We got a tip that one of their North Vietnamese agents claimed to have discovered a site where they were keeping American POWs near Ban Loc in southern North Vietnam. We didn't want to spook the Vietnamese, so while we did send some air reconnaissance over the area, it was too high and there was too much forest to find anything. We needed to send someone in to scout the camp and to meet with the agent. They assigned me.

"I was dropped by a black operations helicopter two kilometers from the meeting site, and when I got there, everything seemed OK—although I thought the agent seemed nervous. But then, I was as nervous as hell, so why shouldn't he be? Still, in retrospect, I should have aborted. He led me right into an ambush, and they had me even before I could swing my rifle up. They stripped me, put a bag over my head, and led me to what sounded like a village or camp. I figured, since we didn't walk for too long, it was Ban Loc. They backed me into this little wooden box and almost dislocated my shoulders pushing me in. I couldn't sit, or stand, or even kneel. It was that small, and it was totally dark—but I could smell incense. The place was totally infused with the smell of sandalwood. After a while, I started to cramp up, and the pain was terrible.

"Then they took me out and beat me with bamboos poles. Then they stuck me back in the box...all still with the hood. This went on for a while, then I get shoved into a chair and felt myself being tied into it. They yanked the bag off my head and started to ask me questions. These weren't the questions you normally think of like 'Who are you?' and 'Why are you here?' but specific questions about people in the unit, about other operations, and so forth. It was clear our ops were blown, and it was obvious to me that I wasn't going to make it out alive because they'd already shown their hand.

"The thing is, there weren't any Vietnamese in the room. They were Russians. They were clean-shaven with short haircuts. I don't know if they were Spetsnaz or KGB, but they were Russians, and they were cruel. One of them had this killing dagger he kept carving on the table with, and about five minutes into the questioning, he puts it up to my cheek and asks me a question. I tell him I don't know, and he pulls the knife down and, well, that was the first scar.

"I could go on about electrodes and such, but suffice it to say it got worse...much worse. I'm glad you don't remember pain, but I sure as hell remember every detail of their sadistic faces as they watched me suffer. And I have lived with the memory of their faces and the reality of my sterility ever since.

"Thad knows this. He also knows how I managed to escape. They questioned me for hours, all the while drinking vodka. They were mostly swigging from the bottle instead of using their glasses. They were mad that I wouldn't talk, so they beat me with the bamboos poles and then called one of the

Vietnamese guards in to the room to put me back in the box. He made a mistake, and instead of backing me in, he put me in headfirst. I could tell from my previous trips in and out that the box had sliding hasp locks at the top and bottom edges of the door. After everything went quiet, I waited a little while longer, and then, because the box was so small and meant to keep me in a squatting position, I realized I could get leverage with my head against the back and with my shoulders against the sides of the box. I managed to get my feet out from under me and against the door. I edged them up, which wasn't as difficult as it might have been, because I was bloody from the beatings and knife cuts, and fresh blood is slippery.

"Well, I got my feet up against the top of the door, and I pushed, using my head and shoulders as leverage, until the first hasp gave way. Then I moved my feet down and pushed against the lower part of the door until the screws holding the second hasp splintered away from the wood. They had tied my hands behind my back, but when I inched backward out of the box, it wasn't hard to get my hands in front of me, because, as I mentioned, all the blood made me slippery. I just sat on the floor and slid my hands under me. Then I took the Russian's killing dagger from the table and cut the cords around my hands. I found my clothes, put them on, and escaped into the dark.

"That's what the Agency knows. I have a whole story about how I escaped while they were in a drunken stupor and passed out, and how I made my way to a pickup point that would be checked daily by our aircraft. That is all true, but what I never told them—or confessed to Thad—was that before I left the house…"

Here J.B. stopped. He took his hands from behind his back and stuck them in the pockets of his pants. His shoulders sank a little, and he dropped his chin, much like a schoolboy about to confess.

He exhaled slowly before he continued. "Just as I remember their faces during the worst part of my ordeal, I remember their faces when I cut their throats. I could give you minute detail, but it is unimportant now. I used the Russian's killing dagger. Before I killed them, I thought about trying to take one of them prisoner, but the logistics were impossible.

"Afterward, I took my clothes, found my dog tags, my watch, the map I had been carrying, and my survival radio. Then I gathered up whatever papers of theirs I could find and took their ID tags and watches. I stuffed everything in a rucksack I found in the room, and then set about causing a distraction and confusion. I used one of their incense punks as a time delay fuse. I lit it and stuck it upright in a pile of cloth I had soaked in vodka and placed between their cots. They had at least four cases of vodka in the house. I threw some clothes in the wooden box after soaking them in vodka, and I poured one or two bottles over their bodies. I figured I had a good hour or so head start before the punk would burn down. And then there would be a fire that had to be dealt with, and after that, confusion about whether I had burned in the house along with the two Russians.

"After I recovered, I naturally gravitated to the CIA. But first there was a lot of to-ing and fro-ing about how the operation had been compromised. We captured the agent who set me up, and he told us he too had been set up and doubled by the Russians. He had agreed to set me up in exchange for them leaving him free. They threatened to kill his family if he didn't follow through working as a double agent for them.

"Then the Agency decided there was a mole who had betrayed us, and there was another full-scale investigation looking for him. They never found anybody during the investigation, but ten years later they uncovered an employee at CIA headquarters who had been spying for the Russians. He had given them the information on the unit and its operations."

J.B. took his hands from his pockets, raising his arms so that his hands made an imploring gesture.

"Hope, I kept thinking you would find someone, marry, and have children. I had too much baggage to ask you to carry it with me. But after a few exploratory visits, I decided we might have at least an occasional relationship if I didn't push too hard. That way, if you did find somebody, letting go wouldn't be too hard—or at least that's what I told myself."

He left the fireplace and went to the drinks table, where he poured a shot glass full of bourbon, downed it, and poured another. As he poured the second glass, he asked rhetorically, "Know what day I got picked up?" He raised the shot glass to eye level, considered it a moment, and raised it farther as if in a toast. "Christmas Eve, December 24, 1971. Tomorrow, it will be forty-two years ago. So, tomorrow I'll be forty-two years old, because that's the day I was reborn. Happy birthday to me." He threw back the second shot and poured a third.

He looked at his companions, both still at opposite ends of the sofa. "No, not that kind of reborn—although the story does tell like the perfect primordial revelation. Road to Damascus and all that. But no, I didn't find Jesus."

"Didn't know he was lost," Thad interjected in an attempt to lighten J.B.'s mood.

"Good one, Thad." J.B. managed a lopsided smile. "No, it was the day Montaigne, Tillich, and Camus crystalized in my brain. Yes, I know I was somewhere between earth and somewhere else...because of the blood loss...but suddenly things became very clear to me. It was on the helicopter ride out of North Vietnam. They had a plasma drip in my arm, and I was lying on a stretcher. I kept asking myself why this had happened. Why had I run into a couple of sadists? The thought pattern was going in big, loopy circles, but midway through one of the loops, something clicked.

"'It happened, stupid. You can't always control what's going to happen, so you have to control how you conduct yourself.' That's Montaigne and the Stoics.

"'But why did it happen?' I asked. 'Did God have some plan in place?'

"That tough part of my brain answered, 'No, there's no plan, Life is what we make of it. We each make our own plan as we each find our individual purpose, choosing our paths from those available. Outside events may beset and bother us, but always we control ourselves.' That's Camus, Montaigne, and a number of the Stoics.

"So, I asked that part of my brain, 'Does that mean there's no God?' And once again I got an immediate answer.

"'No, you dolt! Look around you. Not to believe in some ordering function would be to deny everything you see, smell, feel, or think. Problem is that whatever that ordering function is, it's way beyond your facility to understand. God is an infinite concept while you are a finite being. Attempting to understand what God is, or how he functions, is far beyond your mental capabilities. Accept that there is a God, but realize that he may not involve himself in your daily activities or have a plan for you outside that which naturally occurs in nature. He is not the God of the Torah, of the Bible, of the Koran, or of any number of other texts—for those writings are simply man's attempt to understand what he cannot otherwise explain. Man wishes to understand, but not being able to do so, he relates what he sees and assigns symbols to the events and phenomena.'

"This was from Tillich. It is the cosmic corollary to Montaigne's idea of being unable to govern events. But Tillich also warns us to be careful in choosing a purpose in life. If it is too easily achievable, you risk unhappiness. Therefore, you should seek something that is hard, and perhaps even unmeasurable.

"I asked about a soul, and my mind responded, 'Consider every great and lesser religion, consider man most pagan and even man most primitive—what is the one intrinsic thought that binds them together? A soul. Man is possessed of a soul, and that soul is somehow immortal because it is comprised of energy or some type of life force. Whether it takes one form or morphs constantly is not your concern. Whether it can be saved as an entity is not your concern. What is your concern is that your soul connects you with the infinite. It is that which you cannot understand but that which causes you to exist.'

"By the time they transferred me to the hospital, I had it. My philosophy had become a crystalline entity—fired in a furnace fueled by despair, helplessness, and hate, yet tempered by hope, determination, and a will to live. It was, to my mind, a miracle. In the span of one day, I had achieved the knowledge and understanding that would sustain and guide me through the next three-plus decades. I awoke Christmas Day rejuvenated—knowing not just what I would do, but how I would do it. I would attempt to do the right thing as I saw it, and I would seek to bring happiness to others when I could.

"As you both remember, Christmas has always held exceptional memories for me—in part because of my father's devotion to the holiday—but forty-two years ago, it became, for me, an even more special time of year. The Christmas season became, indeed, my time of primordial spiritual revelation. But sorry, Thad, it didn't involve Jesus."

"No need to be sorry, J.B." Thad spoke quietly. "We've had this discussion before, and we've reached an understanding on your philosophy. But tonight you seem unusually agitated. I'm indeed sorry you didn't previously share the burden of having killed your antagonists, but I understand. Have you reached a crisis of faith? Have you run up against the achievable 'ultimate concern' of which Tillich warned? Have you made too many people happy?"

J.B. sipped at the third shot of bourbon. He walked back to the fireplace, set the glass on the mantel, grabbed the mantel with both hands, and again leaned in toward the fire. After a moment he turned, regarding the tableau as he did. Dug into the right edge of the sofa was the woman he had loved for four decades. She looked concerned, defensive, and more than a little vulnerable. To her right—his left—his best friend of almost fifty years sat dug back into his own corner of the sofa. He too looked concerned. He did not look afraid, for he was sure of his philosophy, but he did seem vulnerable. J.B. knew how much Thad wanted to again become *les trois amis*. He also now knew why Thad had discussed getting the group back together so often lately.

Cancer. Damn! He should have guessed. He had been doing this thing with Thad for eight years now, and other than the occasional mention of J.B.'s trips to New York, they had never really discussed Hope or college. They should be talking about Thad now, not him. Still, he answered.

"Too many people happy? Well, certainly not tonight. Too often, it seems that in trying to help people be happier, I make them less so. Like tonight…the guy at the church. I don't think anything will make him happy. He isn't unhappy about the food, he's unhappy about his status in life…and his expectations are such that he'll always be unhappy. And me challenging him in public…well, that only made him *less* happy.

"I started out working with, and believing in, large groups like the Red Cross and other organized humanitarian efforts. But I soon discovered that, like the government programs I had so staunchly supported in my youth, large groups inevitably get embroiled in politics and power battles."

J.B. paused, then continued. "Yes, Hope, I was the president of the Students for Humphrey campaign; and yes, I believed in the Great Society and all the good it would do. But as I aged, I understood that government can't run programs like that. First and foremost, government makes the assumption that people want what government thinks they want, and that people will respond enthusiastically to what is offered. When you build job training centers, you expect there will be long lines waiting to get in. When there aren't, you build some other program or you provide some sort of subsidy in an effort to get that positive response—not realizing that what you failed to take into account was the fact that in order to reach the job center, a person has to get up at five o'clock and take two buses to the training site. People say, 'That isn't part of my life. I wasn't taught those "getting to work every day" skills, and I have no idea what "personal responsibility" means or why I should care. Why should I work hard when I can get by on what the government already gives me?'

"A couple of years ago, I was helping out our local Christmas effort by handing out Christmas gifts to kids in the county whose parents couldn't afford to buy them presents. We called the effort 'aid to distressed families.' Note that we said 'distressed'—not 'poor' or 'needy' or even 'low income.' Finding the correct label, and ensuring we didn't give offense, was almost as important as the substance of the work. And government regulations—don't get me started! Do you know why so many church groups go to Central America to do clean water projects when right here in Appalachia there are communities without clean water? The EPA and its environmental rules, that's why. There aren't any rules in Honduras—or at least there weren't until recently—so the churches go down there and help them set up clean water projects while kids in Appalachia bathe in polluted water. But I wander too far...

"So, at this Christmas party, this one kid opens his gift, and it's a video game player—but it's not the latest one. He throws a tantrum. I expect his parents to calm him down and explain how last year's player is much better than no player, but the next thing the parents have the player in their hands and they're approaching me and the father starts giving me a hard time about not giving his kid the latest model of the toy. 'Makes him feel poor and underappreciated,' his father says. 'If other kids at his school have parents who give them the latest players, then volunteers should match their efforts.' I tried to explain that the player was in fact new. It wasn't used or reconditioned—it was brand new—but he kept going on about how it wasn't the one they were advertising on television.

"Then, of course, there's the lawsuit. Thad knows about this, but, Hope, you don't." He turned more to face Hope. "I make no-interest micro loans to people in the community. People come to me with an idea, and if I think it's a good one and will help improve the community, I invest startup money in them. Well, I'm now being sued by some people whose ideas I didn't think were all that good. Mostly, their ideas seemed efforts to get money for themselves, so I turned them down. Of course, I know theirs is a nuisance suit, but all the same you'd think you could give your money away without a bunch of people suing you over who you decide to give it to. Their argument is that I should have given them money because they are poor and need it—and since I gave money to other poor people, I'm somehow violating their rights by not giving them the same access to the no-interest loans. They seem to forget the loan part, as in, you must pay the money back…it isn't a gift.

"You know, down on the bayous, my daddy would have taken these people for a boat ride, come home by himself, and the alligators would have taken care of any evidence. But you can't do that in the mountains of Tennessee, in large part because we don't have alligators—and black bears don't eat dead people!

"Yes, Hope, I live in Tennessee, very near the Kentucky border. I live in one of the poorest counties in the country— right smack dab in the middle of Appalachia. I'll tell you why sometime—it's an interesting story—but right now that story is neither here nor there.

"So, until a few minutes ago, I was trying to ask what good does it do to help people who won't help themselves. You want to help people cope with tragedy and loss so they can spring back and become productive members of society again. But so many people today have never been productive members of society—so there is no 'recovering' in the equation. For them, it's all about how much can they get without having to work for it, believing society shortchanged them when they were born and it is society's responsibility to care for them. Or at least it's seeming more and more that way. Still, none of these individual things are problems I cannot deal with. Temporally, they are minor in nature. My larger concern is that somehow the foundation upon which rest my basic beliefs has eroded, and I may fall into the abyss of oblivion, lamenting my life as inadequate instead of accepting that I have done what I could do.

"So, Hope, I don't think I would observe our gathering in the same manner as you. How about…here we are—an ailing but ever-hopeful priest, a somewhat dispirited man for whom being a former spy means little, and a disappointed but highly successful and *très belle femme?*" He smiled as he delivered the French.

"So, *chérie…*" Here, he turned his palms upward as if inviting her to dance. "You are always so *très jolie*, and it breaks my heart to see you sad. What can the good father and I do to undo that which we did unthinkingly or for the wrong reasons?"

She did not respond to his offer to rise and embrace, drawing instead farther back into her den in the corner of the couch.

"Damn you! Don't try to use your spy skills on me! You can't undo all these years with an apology—assuming that *was* an apology!

"Forty years ago, you"—she pointed her finger at Thad—"you convinced me God had died. And you!" She accused J.B. with her eyes, her hand dropping to her lap. "You lived like you were the reincarnation of Camus or Saint-Exupery. I believed you both. You were so solemn and serious. I was convinced God was dead, and I would have to find some purpose to replace him in my life. And that's what I've done. I have my work—at which I'm extremely good. I have my charities and my other good works. So, I'm happy—and then twenty years ago, J.B. begins to sneak back in on his crepe sole shoes…spies do wear crepe sole shoes, don't they?

"And I discover I'm not really happy unless it's when he's visiting, but I don't want to push him away because somehow I felt I pushed him away when I was at Oxford and that's why he joined the army. But, goddamn it—I won't be guilted into thinking the last forty years are my fault!"

Dropping to a knee, J.B. took Hope's hand even though she attempted to pull it away. Grasping it between his hands, he said, "But, *chérie*, I didn't *join* the army. I was drafted. I thought you knew. I sent you a letter telling you my number had come up in the lottery. How can we have spent so much time together in the past twenty years that you didn't know that I didn't march off to the recruiting office because you were seeing who's-his-face, that rugby player?"

For the first time almost rising out of her corner, like a fox checking to see if the hounds are gone, she grabbed her hand back to her chest. "I was not 'seeing' him. I only wrote that he asked me to go to a party after the Oxford-Cambridge match. That's not 'seeing' him. I thought it would make you jealous. But instead you walked out…I can't forgive either of you for walking out of my life the way you did."

Here, Thad decided it was time he had another drink and, rising, went to the drinks table. He selected a bottle of Bacardi, poured a hefty amount into a large glass, and, reaching into the ice bowl, extracted a Coca-Cola. He topped off the rum with coke, took a slice of lime from a saucer, and dropped it into the glass.

"Since we're revisiting our college days, I thought I'd have our old standby." He looked at the glass, then raised it as J.B. had raised his bourdon shot.

"Interestingly, the toast that goes with this drink remains appropriate. *Cuba libre!*" He sipped and returned to his seat.

Quiet descended once more upon the room. In other circumstances, the crackling of the fire might have broken the mood, but it was a gas fire in front of which J.B. stood once more, and it just silently flickered. Hope held her crystal scotch glass in two hands in front of her face, either as a kaleidoscope through which she was viewing the scene or to create a mirrored maze through which others would have to find their way to reach her. Thad tried to look more composed, spreading his left arm over the back of the sofa and laying his right, drink in hand, on the bolster-like leather arm.

"You know, Hope, you sound a lot like my mother did forty years ago. Since I had no brothers or sisters, my entering the seminary ended any chance she had of grandchildren. Since my father had died the year before, when I chose the priesthood, I essentially left her on her own. It took a while, but she eventually came to understand that being a priest isn't a profession like being a lawyer or doctor. It's not an occupation like pilot or ditchdigger, and it isn't something you necessarily choose. It chooses you.

"For others, there are decisions to make. Should you teach? Should you go on to graduate school? Should you be an editor, and if so, should you work on magazines? Books? Newspapers, perhaps? Maybe advertising? Maybe art? You had all these choices. For me there was only one choice. Would I accept the calling tugging me toward the priesthood; for being a priest is truly a vocation. Yes, there are far too many who choose it for the wrong reasons, and even those of us who are called for valid reasons always fight through doubt—but a *good* priest is always one who is called to the cloth.

"Believe me, had you not been in Oxford, I would have discussed my decision with you in such detail that you would have been nauseated and begged me to stop. It was that difficult—J.B. knows. We spent entire nights in the apartment dissecting the issue until there was no meat left on the skeleton. Then J.B. got his draft notice, and I was on my own.

"As for convincing you that God was dead...I realized I was attempting to resist the call I was feeling. If I could prove God was dead, then the call I was hearing was only an echo of things past. I could rationalize ignoring it. Eventually I failed. Unfortunately, it was after you left. Perhaps I should have sent you a postcard." Here Thad made a gesture as if writing in air: "'Hope, it's all a mistake. God's alive.' What would you have done?

"Well, Miss Hope, I don't think it would have come as a surprise, because I don't think that in your heart you ever really accepted any of the 'God is dead' arguments I presented. I think you've always believed God is part of your life. Just this evening you've called upon him three times to damn J.B."

Leaning toward her but never letting go of his anchor on the back of the sofa, he said, "I think you should be careful what you ask, for J.B. teeters on the precipice. As it is, I expect he'll do some time in purgatory, for our boy has not led the holiest of lives—although the last ten years or so will significantly propitiate his earlier lapses. You don't mind me saying that, do you, J.B.?"

J.B., who was seemingly elsewhere in his mind, responded, "No, I guess not." He waited a moment, then, as if he was expected to say something else, he added, "If you're expecting something witty, I'm all out of wit for the evening. But I'm glad we've all had our say."

He walked to the window and, stepping between the drapes, almost disappeared into the window well. The quiet descended once more, and the room seemed a theater stage frozen midscene. At last the quartz carriage clock on the mantel broke the spell, striking two. None had heard it before.

Then, as if cued by the clock, J.B. emerged, leaving the curtains slightly askance, and announced, "It's sleeting out. It will be too dangerous to go back to the District tonight. I'll arrange rooms for you here. I think we all need to sleep on what has been said and think about what might be said later. Besides, it's two o'clock, and we've passed out of the hours of reflectors and philosophers into the time of thieves, spies, and ne'er-do-wells. I've spent far too much of my life skulking around between midnight and dawn to expect anything good to happen at this hour."

He picked up the phone and punched the button for the desk. Even at two o'clock in the morning, there was an immediate response, and although the inn was full, the receptionist knew that there were always one or two service rooms held back for unanticipated visits by valued clients. These were readied for Hope and Thad. At 2:15 a.m., a bellman cleared the tables from J.B.'s suite while the on-duty manager escorted the two exhausted friends to their beds. J.B. lay awake on his own bed for less than a minute before falling into the sleep of a troubled man.

It wasn't long before he felt as if he had awoken, but he knew he was still asleep—or at least he thought he was still asleep—although he might not have been, for he sensed the coldness of the room. He felt a presence, and yet there was no one there; but still he expected to hear whatever-it-was speak, and he was not surprised when it did.

"Hello, J.B." There was no corporality to this ghost, just a sense of presence. No cloak or hood, no plasma or smoke, just the voice of a second individual with whom he was conversing.

For someone who had only a few years earlier finally expelled two particularly sadistically smiling demons from his sleep, the Ghost of Christmas Present (as the presence introduced itself) proved somewhat problematic. It sounded suspiciously like the part of his brain with which he had held the conversation in the helicopter, although there was a greater solemnity with this voice. The voice he heard on the helicopter had been one of command. This voice was softer, more hollow somehow. Not sad but not happy.

J.B. was not sure he wanted to respond to this voice. At the moment he wanted very much to be pessimistic and dismiss it. Tell it to go away. Feeling sorry for himself would relieve him of responsibility. Sometimes it just felt so good to give up. Good in a bad sort of way. It was like the hurting that came after a football game or rugby match. You could get in an ice bath and then have a deep tissue massage, both in themselves unpleasant activities, or you could just lie there and give in to it. Sometimes, especially after a loss, you wanted to hurt. You wanted to feel bad. It somehow justified the loss and provided an excuse not to go back to the 'normal' world just yet. The pain was propitiation for the sin of losing. Still, the voice was persistent.

GHOST: "Hard evening to deal with, wasn't it?"

J.B.:   "It had to be done. Things have to be said. Time is too short. Thad could be dying."

GHOST: "You didn't know that before tonight. Until a little while ago, this was all about you. You'd lost faith that you'd been doing the right thing, and you wanted external validation that you'd made the right choices in your life. Well, you can't have it. That's not how life works. You seldom remember your successes, choosing to dwell on your failures. Each time you think about what you think is a failure, it becomes larger in your mind so that eventually those thoughts push out everything else, and you feel a failure overall."

J.B.:   "Not true. I do remember my successes. How else would I gauge my failures?"

GHOST: "No, you don't really remember your successes; you just remember the validation you received from them and the lack of validation from your failures. Perhaps some of what you perceive as failures were, in fact, successes. Just because someone doesn't run up and wrap their arms around your neck doesn't mean you've failed, and just because they do doesn't mean you've succeeded in other than a momentary fashion. I thought you had dealt with this in college. Camus over Dostoyevsky, purpose and free will over despair, and pre-determination caused by class and society."

It seemed that the ghost paused to think.

GHOST: "You don't know how lucky you are in that I'm a ghost who understands the liberal arts. Can you imagine this discussion if I were an engineer or scientist? There'd be little hope for you."

J.B.:   "Hope is part of the question, your little joke aside. I have indeed toyed with her all these years, rationalizing away offering her a commitment. Still, I don't think she wants to leave New York, and I definitely can't live there. I doubt she would be happy in Tennessee, so I suppose we take what we can get, which is little bits here and there."

GHOST: "But you've never asked her to live in Tennessee. You just assumed she wouldn't and assumed that if you suggested it, you would somehow change the dynamic of the relationship for the worse. Pretty cowardly, and more than a little selfish, don't you think? You have a casual long-distance relationship that is an on-off affair in your mind. But what is it in Hope's mind? Does she want more, less, or what you have? What is her rationalization for allowing things to muddle on? Isn't this like wanting to feel bad? You want to justify yourself to yourself. Well, in a way, I'm yourself, and I'm not going to let you do it. So there!"

J.B.: "Why is life so hard?"

GHOST: "Oh no, you don't! We're not going to go through that crappy canard again. Your life isn't hard. It's privileged. Even the hard things you've done, the dangerous things, the stupid things, are things only a very few people get to experience. People write novels about what you did to earn your daily bread. And speaking of daily bread, you've accumulated the resources to buy quite a bit of that. No, my friend, you can't ask that question, because life isn't hard. Not for you."

J.B.: "So...if life isn't hard, why does this seem so difficult? Why can't I dispel the loss of validation I feel?"

GHOST: "OK, one more time. You have led an exceptional life. Exceptional in that you created opportunities to do things other people just dream of. You have done them well. Some better than others. Perhaps you're simply wanting the validation of Hope and Thad. Ever thought of that? Perhaps this whole thing is your way of expressing a guilty feeling that you've misled and/or abandoned the true friends of your youth. God knows you can't have friends in the CIA, and you certainly can't have friends abroad where everybody is a possible adversary in one form or another. Maybe you're just tired of being alone and need someone with whom you can share life."

J.B.:   "Maybe. You think?"

Ghost: "J.B., the question is, do *you* think? Remember, life is what you make it. Within the physical confines dictated by your health and wealth, you make the decisions that determine what you do and how you do it. Some people exist in another world that is solely within their minds because they can't handle the real world. Others dream, and their dreams make them sad. Some are sad and don't know why. Many are angry that 'life' has treated them as it has, and they don't know how to find their way out of the morass. Those, however, who take responsibility for themselves are able to find happiness and satisfaction. It isn't easy and requires a great deal of effort at first, but like anything else, it becomes second nature after a while. Like riding a bike or hitting a ball or, in your case, assessing a target personality as a potential spy. You just do it."

J.B.:   "That's a bit too much like Professor Pangloss, which, of course, was Voltaire's little dig at Leibnizian Optimism."

The back part of J.B.'s mind was trying valiantly to insert some rationality into this otherwise irrational episode.

J.B.:   "Still, I guess if you're going to be alive, it's better to be an optimist than a pessimist. Pretty simple without going into all the metaphysics reaching that conclusion requires. Although one must be a realist as well. I suppose this is where taking personal responsibility enters the equation."

Here J.B. would have looked at the ghost had the latter exhibited any corporeal reality. Once again, the silence in J.B.'s mind gave rise to a feeling the ghost was thinking, and then...

GHOST: "At the risk of overstating the obvious—damn straight! It's all about personal responsibility. You know what the right thing is. Do it. You know where you want to be. Go there. You know about all this. Stop procrastinating!"

J.B.: "And what if Thad dies?"

GHOST: "Hell, J.B., we all die. If Thad dies, you'll be sad, but he's prepared to die. Shouldn't you help him be happy for whatever time remains to him?"

J.B.: "You sound as if he will die from this."

GHOST: "This or that. He could get hit by a car going home from the hotel. He might decide to take his own life rather than suffer the pain of slowly dying of cancer. I don't know. I'm the Ghost of Christmas Present. There is no Ghost of Christmas Future because the future hasn't happened yet. You and your friends have yet to make it happen."

J.B.: "You're right. We do make our own futures, don't we? The only thing predetermined is that at some point, we die. How we live is within our own control. Our way of addressing reality is what's important. Glass half full and all that. Damn! The thoughts are so simple. Why isn't the execution?"

GHOST: "Because if it was, you wouldn't place any value on it. Happiness isn't a permanent state of being. It comes in small measure. A smile, a glance, a warm feeling, a laugh, a feeling of loving and being loved—that's happiness. It isn't there constantly, but it's there a lot more often if you're open to the possibilities of life. You don't search for happiness, because it's elusive. Rather, it finds you, sometimes in the most unlikely places and times."

J.B.:   "Yes, it does seem so."

GHOST: "So, glad we had this chat. Get on with it."

J.B.:   "Wait. I'm not done. I have all sorts of questions I want to discuss! Like what is the purpose of life?"

GHOST: "The purpose of life? J.B., you might as well ask why the seas are boiling hot and whether pigs have wings. It's time. You're on your own again. Don't make this a wasted visit."

The curtains stirred as if being parted by an entity exiting the room. Sunlight came through the opening. J.B. sat on the side of his bed, sunlight on his face. He walked to the window well and opened the curtains. Blue sky overhead, no ice on the streets. The carriage clock on the mantel indicated it was almost a quarter after nine. As he turned toward the bathroom, his room phone rang.

"Hello?"

"Good morning, Mr. Le Roi." It was the front desk calling. "Ms. Merriweather asked me to tell you she has a table in the dining room for ten o'clock and to ask would you and Father Cawthorne please join her."

"Ten o'clock. Yes." J.B. smiled. "Ah, could you please have Frank wait on us? That is if he's working today."

"Of course, Mr. Le Roi. Frank is working today, and I'm sure he would very much like to wait your table."

J.B. placed the phone back in its cradle. He felt different this morning and, emerging a few minutes later from the shower, he felt even better. He knew what to do and how to do it.

The small dining room, which was on the roof of the hotel, had more than a few occupants when he arrived. It was elaborately decorated for Christmas—a large tree in one corner, wreaths hung in the large, paned windows. Red hothouse roses with green holly accentuated the ironed white, linen tablecloths.

Hope sat at a table for four that was lit indirectly by the low rays of sunlight through the large windows. The angle of the sun created elongated shadows, making the room seem larger than it was. Frank, a red rosebud in the lapel of his immaculate white waiter's jacket, hovered about his waiter's station, watching the door for J.B.'s entrance. Frank was a fixture of the hotel, and J.B. liked to interact with him. Frank was always cheerful, and J.B. had asked for Frank so that his own—that is, J.B.'s—cheerfulness would be reciprocated by at least one person this morning.

As he started across the dining room, Thad touched his elbow from behind. J.B. turned, a smile on his face, only to be greeted by a larger smile on Thad's face. Their eyes locked briefly, and J.B. saw in Thad's a happiness he had not seen since college.

They approached Hope from either side, each offering her a kiss on the cheek, which she returned appropriately.

As they sat, Frank was there with the sterling silver coffeepot, filling the cups.

Out of the slanting sun rays, J.B. could now see Hope's face. He thought, "Her smile is far stronger than the winter sun."

Reaching out her hands to either side, Hope grasped J.B.'s with her right and Thad's with her left. "Good morning," she said. "I thought you two were going to sleep forever. I've already been out for a walk." Her cheeks showed evidence of a walk in the thirtysomething temperatures. She continued. "I slept marvelously. J.B., it must have been that Sazerac, because I had the most remarkable dream."

Thad leaned forward. "So did I. Most remarkable dream I've ever had. Almost a revelation dream, you might say." He paused, then continued. "Do you remember what our grandmothers used to say about dreams?"

It took but a moment before Hope bubbled out, "You mean, if you tell a dream before breakfast, it will come true? Then I certainly want to tell mine now!"

"Me too!" Thad said, squeezing her hand.

Frank approached the table, ready to take their orders.

J.B. looked into his smiling face and said, "Frank. For the time being, please just keep the cups filled. I think it might be some time before we're ready for breakfast."

It truly was the best season of the year.

The Pickle Jar

"Twelve...thirteen...fourteen..." He stacked the quarters in columns of four as he counted them out. "Eighteen...nineteen...twenty..." He placed a ruler next to the twenty stacks of quarters on his left and then started again. "One...two...three..." When he finished with the quarters, he moved on to the dimes, and then the nickels and pennies. These stacks were to his right.

"Not bad. More than forty-five dollars this month," he said aloud as if to reassure himself of the total.

After he had finished the counting, he reloaded his change-maker with quarters, dimes, nickels, and pennies from the stacks on the right, and then, leaving the twenty stacks of quarters to the left, he began to roll the other coins into paper tubes. As he loaded a tube, he would fold the top closed and place the tube on the right side of his desk. Since each tube held a specific number of coins, he would always end the session with too few coins to fill another tube. These he swiped into the one-gallon pickle jar that was his bank. It was filled with one-dollar bills, some fives, one or two tens, and numerous tubes of quarters, nickels, dimes, and pennies. The half-dollars and silver dollars he kept separate in a mason quart jar. These were silver coins, and he didn't want to use them in his daily business of selling newspapers. These were his "savings account," for he reckoned that in a few years, silver would be worth more per ounce, so he could sell the coins as silver and get more than their face value. At least he hoped it would happen.

Now he rolled the stacks of quarters on his left into their own tubes. These he would take to the bank and exchange for a twenty-dollar bill that he would present to his father. "To help with the utilities," he would say. He did this every month without fail. He never left the money on a counter or table. It was always, "To help with the utilities," he would say, handing the bill directly to his father, who accepted it solemnly and replied with a stoic, "Thank you."

His parents hadn't needed the extra money until his father became ill and couldn't work a full day. He had what people called a wasting disease. He was slowly wasting away, and it didn't seem to make any difference what the doctors did; he continued to look weaker month by month, sometimes even day by day, for he, as all sick people, had his good days and his bad days.

His mother worked full time as a secretary, but her pay didn't cover all the expenses, especially the medical costs the health insurance didn't cover. They had already gone through their savings.

"Mickey, please come and help me with this table?" His father called him from the dining room, where he was setting up his temporary office. "I want to move the table more over by the window so I'll have some natural light and I'll be able to use the floor lamp without having to trail the wire across the walking area. Don't want to trip on it if I'm dragging my feet."

Mickey pulled the large table closer to the window. It was no effort for him, although the mahogany table weighed a couple of hundred pounds. Mickey was always referred to as a "strapping lad," and, at fourteen, almost six feet tall and 170 pounds, he looked almost twenty. That is, if you looked at him from a distance, for while he had the body of a twenty-year-old, his face made him look more like a cherub than an Adonis. The girls were still calling him cute, although a girl in the junior class had asked him to the Sadie Hawkins dance.

"Dad," Mickey asked as he moved the chairs to places along the wall of the dining room, "do you really think you should keep working like this?"

"And what would I be doing otherwise?" His father's voice sounded just the least bit exasperated. "I suppose I could just sit in a rocker on the front porch looking for the reaper to come strolling along the sidewalk, and then I could invite him up on the porch for a glass of iced tea and some conversation. No, that's not for Sean O'Hara. I've been working since I was eleven years old, and I want you to remind your mother when I keel over here at the table, she's to bill the client for the time before I passed. You'll remember that now, won't you, Mickey?" He sounded sincere, although a twinkle flashed quickly across his otherwise drawn face.

"Yes, sir. I'll remember."

Mickey went back to the bedroom he had, until last June, shared with his older brother Cormac. But now it was his alone, for Cormac had joined the army upon graduation from high school. He was in infantry training at Fort Benning, Georgia. He had wanted to go to college, but with the family financial situation being what it was, he had joined the army to take advantage of the GI Bill. After a few years of soldiering, he said, he would be able to have his tuition and books paid for, and, with a part-time job, it would be just as if he had received a scholarship to go to college. Besides, Old Sean, his grandfather, and Sean, his father, had both served in the army in the two wars, and O'Haras had fought in the Civil War as well, so it was his duty to "join up," as he put it.

Their father would sometimes tell stories that Old Sean had heard from his father, who had fought in that Civil War.

"It was strange," his father said. "There were Irish regiments fighting for the North and Irish regiments fighting for the South. Sometimes they would be fighting each other, hurling curses in Gaelic back and fought across the parapets. Who you fought for was determined by where you came into the country and settled." Mickey's people had landed in South Carolina and then later had moved to the Mississippi Territory, where they bought land and became farmers. But after a couple of generations, the land had been so divided up among the various O'Hara sons, there wasn't any left for Old

Sean's generation, so the O'Haras moved to town and became merchants, policemen, and bookkeepers.

Mickey hadn't given much thought to whether he would "join up" or not. Right now, his mother needed his help to make ends meet around the house, and besides, he was only a freshman in high school. He had another three years before he had to decide. His grades were good—way better than Cormac's—so maybe he would win a scholarship to one of the local colleges where he could live at home, help his mother, work part time, and still get a college education. "And speaking of colleges..." he said to himself.

He took the small ledger from the desk drawer and added twenty-five dollars to his balance. "I think it's time to buy it," he thought, "but how long will it take me to just make the money back if I do buy it?"

The "it" he referenced was a new portable typewriter. With a portable typewriter, he could work during study hall producing term papers for more people. Right now, he was limited to using his father's Royal Standard, and that was only when his father wasn't using it to produce reports and invoices for his clients. It was a large heavy machine that, as of this morning, sat on the dining room table, where Mickey had carried it for his father.

"With a portable that has magic touch margins and a full-sized keyboard and automatic double-spacing, I can do more papers for more people, and more people means more money. And college students do longer papers than high schoolers, so that's more per paper." The thought that most of the money he made came from selling paper, whether it was newspapers on street corners in the morning or pages of typing paper prepared as term papers, made him chuckle.

That chuckle buoyed his spirit, which had dipped momentarily when he thought of seeing the pickle jar empty of its rolls of coins and folded bills. Sometimes he worried that he was becoming too obsessed with making money. That he too much enjoyed seeing the pickle jar fill up with change and dollar bills. But then he reassured himself that being independent was not a bad thing and that being independent meant you paid your own way.

"Old Sean worked his entire life," he mused, "as did his father and his father's father." Work was just the natural order of things, and you worked to make the money you needed to live, so the more he worked, the better off he would be. "At least, that is what I observe to be the case," he thought. "My father will die in a year or two, maybe less, but he is at the table working so that my mom doesn't have to take a second job."

He took the bills from the pickle jar and added their total. Then he began reaching for the rolls of coins, adding up the total roll by roll, first all the quarter rolls, then the dimes and so forth. When he reached the amount he needed, the pickle jar was all but empty. At least he had not had to reach into the mason jars for any silver dollars.

Instead of riding his bike downtown, he took the bus. First, he stopped at the bank to redeem the rolls of coins for bills and the smaller bills for larger ones. When he had the cash, he went to the stationery store, where, to his surprise, they had a 10 percent off sale.

"I should have thought of asking about sales the last time I was in," he thought. "Well, lesson learned." On the bus ride back, he considered that while the portable was, indeed, portable, it was still heavy. But the basket on his bicycle would carry the case nicely.

"Now I need to have some flyers printed so I can put them up on the bulletin boards at the local colleges. I wonder if I can get that done for the 10 percent I saved. Probably…well, maybe…sure! I'm being lucky today, so I think it'll work." And it did, for when he left the print shop on Washington Avenue, he still had ten one-dollar bills in his pocket, which, of course, would go back into the pickle jar. "Too bad dollar bills aren't like rabbits or gerbils," he said to himself. "That would be nice."

At home, he carefully set up the portable and began to practice typing. He adjusted the touch control and set the margins to one inch, which were the normal margins for educational papers. He had to be careful not to strike the keys with too much pressure, because the distance the key traveled to make the print bar strike the roller was much less than it was on his father's standard machine.

He found himself typing even faster than his normal sixty-five words a minute. He enjoyed it. He had been typing and playing the piano since he was six. At first it was a chore, but the better he became, the more he liked it. It was his father's idea. His father had typed his way through North Africa, Italy, and France with the US Army. When he had joined the army, he was trained as a rifleman until his company commander discovered that he not only could type, but he could also type fast and accurately. Then, the battalion commander had seen him, and then division commander, and finally he was running an administrative section for Third Army Headquarters. In 1941, he had been a private; in 1945, he was a master sergeant, and it was all because he could type. "And take shorthand," Mickey thought. "And take shorthand."

So, Cormac and Mickey had learned to type, take shorthand, and play the piano at an early age. "The piano is good for finger strength," their father had said.

"And it is," Mickey thought. "But not so good for baseball or football, because I can't afford to risk getting a finger broken." He longed to play those sports, but he had to find other ways to compete and stay in shape, so he ran. He wasn't particularly fast, but he could run forever. That meant he ran cross-country on the high school's cross-country team and for the longer distance runs on the track team. Runs where you could watch the start, go get a hot dog and a Coke, chat a while with friends, and then come back for the finish.

He had to be careful, though, to balance his time so that such things did not interfere with his ability to fulfill his typing commitments; but still, he would earn his letterman's sweater on the cross-country and track teams. "And girls like lettermen..." he thought. "Girls like lettermen." And there was that girl in his algebra class, the one with the chestnut hair and the blue eyes. "I'll bet she likes lettermen. Well, we'll see." The thought pleased him. He stopped typing long enough to imagine himself in the blue sweater. "No, wait! If she likes let-termen and she likes me, then she'll be the one wearing the blue sweater."

Yes, he could see it now. She is wearing his blue sweater with the gold *M*, and they're holding hands. He can see it plainly in his mind's eye. They're actually holding hands. And then the thought struck him, "But then I'll have to buy her a pin or a lavaliere necklace, and there will be dates…that means money for movies, hamburgers, Cokes…and presents at Christmas and on her birthday…Christmas!" He sat up straighter in his chair. "Jesus, Mary, and Joseph! Christmas is two months away, and I'm all but broke. And me thinking of girlfriends!"

He quickly pulled the practice page from the typewriter roller and took out the folder in which he kept his clients' papers to be typed. He would type a paper and then get to the colleges and put up his flyers. "I'm going to need lots of new clients," he thought as he glanced at the almost empty pickle jar.

A Dog of Many Names

Maybe just a wink or two more, here in front of the fire. This new hearthrug is *really* thick and...*so* soft. *Mmmm!* I could lie here all night and not have to walk back to my bed. I bet that bedroom is cold...maybe just a minute or two more...

No! I have a job to do and...*ohhh* yes...this downward dog stretch is...*ahhh*! That's better. Now let's stre-e-etch the neck up. Right! Reach for the ceiling...Oh my! Was that a crack I heard? Hope not! Oh well...let's just plop down for a moment and get things in the proper perspective...

Oh hello! Didn't see you there. Reading, are you? Good thing. I'd read if I could, but holding books is difficult. You know, the whole "no thumb" business. So you just read on there...

My name is Jack. I live with Anne and Tony, a couple of retired spies who came back to Anne's hometown in Tennessee to settle down after wandering the world doing whatever it is spies do in something they call the "Great Game." Tony, Anne, and I live in a house near the top of Black Oak Ridge, which looks out over the Cumberland Mountains. Anne and Tony built the house, which is kind of where this whole thing started.

As a puppy, I lived with some people who thought I was somewhat of a burden, and the man was always waving a stick at me. A couple of times, he even swatted me with it. It hurt. When I was nine months old, the man took me for a ride. I like riding in cars. But this time, the next thing I knew, I was by myself in the woods with the car driving off down the road. It was early in December, and the temperature had started to drop into the twenties at night, so I needed to find a warm place to sleep. That and something to eat.

Over the next few days, I learned to fend for myself chewing sticks, drinking from streams, and eating warm deer poop. (Oops. Guess that may be a little too much information, but hey, it's a way to stay alive in the winter what with all the small animals already hibernating and the ground birds being out of season and such.)

Anyway, a few weeks later, I saw these guys up on the ridge, and they'd got a big fire going in a fifty-gallon drum, so I sort of sauntered up—nonchalant-like, but wary, of course, for things being thrown at me or people chasing me with sticks. No one seemed to mind, so I settled down near the drum and got warm for the first time in what seemed forever. It was nice. Now, I know you may think you know what "nice" means, but after almost two weeks in the cold, this was *nice*!

When the sun went down and the builders went home, they let the fire burn down, but the drum stayed warm for a few hours. I still needed somewhere to stay out of the wind, so

I found a place under the plastic sheeting they were using to wrap the floor joists. (See, hanging around these builders, I was picking up the lingo of the trade. I knew about concrete forms and framing and such...)

After a couple of days, a new pickup truck comes driving up the hill. The driveway is still just a really steep gravel track, and you have to use four-wheel drive to get up to the top. So anyway, these two people get out of the truck. He's normal height, gray hair, nothing remarkable—although I detect a slight limp when he walks on uneven ground. She's a blonde—very attractive, and if not bubbly, then maybe just a little lively. They seem nice enough people and not like someone who's going pick up a stick and wave it at you. So, I meander over, tail wagging, you know, and say hello. The guy actually kneels down and pets me. The lady makes nice noises but doesn't offer her hand, so I stand up and walk over to her just so she'll have the chance to pet me. Well, she does just that, a quick pat on the head, and then the builder is there, grabbing their hands and taking them over to the foundation and basement he poured for the house. He keeps going on about how it's only a sixteenth of an inch off over eighty-five feet, so I get the impression that's important.

Naturally I follow along. When they stop, I stop and sit. If they stay in one place too long, I lie down but always within an arm's reach. At one point, the guy reaches down and starts to rub my belly. It's the first serious belly rub I've ever had, and it feels really good. I mean, like really, *really* good. Then the lady says, "Is this the kind of dog you've talked about?"

The guy, rubbing my belly all the time, says, "Maybe. But you know we're in an apartment that doesn't allow pets, and besides, he probably belongs to one of the building crew."

Darn! It had looked really promising, but as they say, timing is everything. At least the contractor told them I wasn't there with any of the crew. Just a dog, he said, that showed up a couple of days ago, maybe from the horse farm in the valley.

So now they're going to leave. I beat them to the truck, and, again, tail wagging, wait for someone to open the door. He tells her to stand with me while he turns the truck around because he doesn't want to run over me. I sit nicely as he maneuvers the truck in the tight space. But then the lady gets in, and they start down the hill. They have to go slow because it's so steep. I decide, what the heck—nothing ventured, nothing gained. So I head down the hill after them. Now, I can see the guy is watching me in his door mirror, and the lady is watching me too, in the passenger-side mirror. As they reach the bottom of the hill and turn onto the flat part of the gravel drive, the truck begins to go faster. Now I'm running full out, trying to catch it. My ears are flapping, and my tongue's hanging out. Hey! *You* try catching a truck that's going down a 900-foot hill and then a 1,000-foot road through a glen…and having to run on rocks to do it!

About halfway out of the glen, I see the lady turn to the guy and say something, and the truck actually skids to a stop on the gravel. The lady gets out and opens the wing door—it's one of those "king cab" pickups. As I reach the truck, it's just a natural jump, and I'm in the back! I sniff a couple of times around the back seat and then put my front feet on the center console, lick the guy's ear, and put my chin on his shoulder. The lady gets back in the truck, and off we go.

Now, dogs and trucks are made for each other, but I have to say this was something new for me. I had no idea where we were going, but we were going, and there was this warm air blowing in my face from the dash vents. We were off on our first adventure.

So the man turns his head and, looking across my nose, says to the lady, "Why would Miss 'I've Never Had a Dog in My Life' tell me to stop the truck?"

"Well," she says, "you always told me that you don't choose the dog, the dog chooses you; and, sweetheart, even a blind person could see this dog has chosen you. What are we going to call him?"

And so, my first and forever name became "Jack."

They stop at Walmart and buy me a crate, a collar, a leash, two bowls, and several small bags of dog food, to see—Tony says—which one I take to. Now, are those great people or what?

Then we go to the vet. The vet tells them I'm nine months old and in really good shape for having been living in the woods...although I've got just a little frostbite on the tips of my ears. The vet guesses I'm part Lab and part border collie. Now, I don't know about any of that because I don't really remember my mom or any of my siblings, but I do like to herd things, I can jump straight up, and I swim like a champ, so maybe the vet got it right. A couple of shots, and then the vet hangs these two tags on my brand-new red collar. (Sure, I'm color blind like every other dog, but Anne kept telling me how handsome I looked in my new red collar, so either she was lying or I had a red collar.) Then Tony says we need something to tell people my name and who to call if I get lost, so he goes out and brings back another tag that says "Jack," and he hangs that on the collar.

Honest people that they are, Anne and Tony put ads in the local newspapers announcing they found me in the vicinity of Bacon Springs, and for a week, every time the phone rings, I see Tony blanch a little just before he answers. Twice I hear him say, "I'm sorry. I don't think the one we found is yours, but I hope you find your dog."

This is all just before Christmas, so Anne starts telling Tony he doesn't need any more presents because he has "Jack the Christmas Dog." I kind of like that...the Christmas Dog. It has a certain *je ne sais quoi*, don't you think?

On Christmas Eve, I keep hearing things outside that make me a little nervous, so I get up to shake and then lie down again several times. Well, unknown to me, the people upstairs (I was in my crate downstairs) keep hearing my collar tags jingle and think they are hearing Santa's reindeer. They are talking about it on Christmas morning over the Christmas stollen and coffee when I walk into the dining room and jingle for them. It's amazing how like jingle bells three aluminum tags can sound when you shake them vigorously together. Everyone stops talking and looks at me.

"Well," Anne says, just a little disappointed, "it wasn't reindeer at all. It was Jack the Jingle Dog welcoming Christmas." Jingle Dog doesn't have the same panache as Christmas Dog, but don't they say about the only thing worse than people talking about you is people not talking about you?

Now, while we are waiting to see if anyone claims me, we take walks in the woods on the ridge near where the house is being built. I tear off running at full speed, ears back, tongue out. I know it looks like I might never come back, but I'm very careful to run figure eights, always crossing back over their path every few minutes so I'll know where they are. I'm not about to run away or get lost. I mean, I may be slow (that's a joke, people, because I'm *really* fast), but even if I don't remember her, Momma didn't raise no dummy! I love running but no way am I going to lose my new family.

On one occasion as I run by Tony, I hear Anne say, "Whoosh!" The next thing you know, they've hung the sobriquet "Jack the Whoosh Dog" on me, and sometimes it's just Whoosh Dog. Sobriquet? Come on, you know. That's French for kind of a nickname. Hey, I could have said epithet instead of sobriquet, which would have tilted this story in a more classical direction, since as many of you are aware, all the great Greek warriors and gods were possessed of epithets, like Hector of the Shining Helm or Zeus the Cloud Gatherer. Although, of course, Hector was a Trojan. (We're educated in our family. Tony and Anne speak French, Arabic, and Italian, and I handle the animal languages, although an incident a couple of years ago showed I'm a little weak when it comes to communicating with skunks! Boy, was *that* ever an adventure. And oh, by the way, that old saying about skunk smell and tomato juice…it isn't true. It's just got to wear off.)

A few days after Christmas, we start back to Washington because, as Tony puts it, "If you've lost a dog this good and you haven't checked the newspapers or put up any fliers, you don't deserve him." That makes me feel good. I have to say that 500 miles is a long way to go in a car, but as Tony says, "The adventure continues," and boy, did it ever!

So, Tony and Anne lived in this penthouse in Virginia overlooking the Potomac River. Twelve stories up. And since they have to sneak me in, we have to use the stairs. Now, I saw a stair or two before I left Tennessee, but twelve floors? Come on! This is where I learn that not all adventures are pleasant ones. It takes several attempts, but I finally manage after Tony carries me a few times. Think about it. You have to go…I mean, *have* to go, but first you've got to walk down twelve floors and then through a tunnel to get to the outside. Then there are these little grass strips with cars whizzing by all the time, and for the longest time, it was mainly the cars doing the whizzing because I was too scared and distracted. Boy, do cats have it easy or what?

After a few days, Tony decides we'll use the elevator. So we go down the hall, and, good dog that I am, I sit nicely in this little alcove. Then there's this noise, and these doors open, and Tony steps forward. I, of course, being the smart one of the duo, have no intention of advancing into that confined space and allowing those doors to trap me, so I just sit there. I don't move, and when Tony does that little tug thing with the leash, I just lie down. So then he picks me up and we ride the elevator.

It takes a while, but I become an accomplished elevator rider, median strip user, and ignorer of all cars that threaten my concentration during those moments on the median. Chasing balls on the tennis courts, ignoring those other dogs on our walks...wow! I had no idea apartment living was such a challenge. Each time there's something new, it's an adventure. So Tony dubs me "Jack the Adventure Dog," as in, "Well, Adventure Dog, are you ready for another foray into the wilds of downtown Arlington, Virginia?"

After what seems forever, we move back to Tennessee and into our new house. Each time I come in from the outdoors, I whoosh to find Tony, and when I find him, I bound into the room and leap so that I turn in midair, landing with my back to him in a sitting position. Then I back left and right until I touch his leg. We call this "scooching," and I scooch with the best. In fact, I'm so good, Tony starts calling me the Scooch Dog. Sometimes I may miss on the jump by as much as three feet, but I always scooch into position. Tony says I need a back-up indicator. I guess he means one of those beep, beep things trucks use.

Now we have a morning routine where Tony and I get up, or rather, where I get up and then wake Tony. All these tags on my collar make a perfect alarm, and I'm always within two minutes of the clock when I shake them to get him up. If he doesn't move, I wait a few minutes and then do it again. If that still doesn't work, I sit beside the bed and laser him with my superdog look. That gets him every time, and he always says to Anne, "Well, the Alarm Dog just went off, so I guess I have to get up."

We empty the dishwasher, putting the dishes away from the night before. He feeds me my breakfast, and then we take two cups of coffee into the bedroom, where he and Anne discuss things like religion, physics, philosophy, family, and such. I usually just take nap Alpha while I wait for them to finally get moving. (Nap Alpha? You know that's the one after breakfast. Then nap Bravo is the one after lunch, and nap Charlie is the one we take after dinner and before we go to bed.) I definitely don't sleep, though, when they talk football—which they do a lot, because Tony has taken up coaching middle school football.

Secretly, I know he wishes he was down the road coaching at Sewanee. Now, even though Tony is a Sewanee grad, I can't really root for the team because, I mean, after all, they're the Tigers, and you know…it's that Dogs and Cats thing. Even the high school team here in Oak Ridge is the Wildcats. What's going on? Do you realize that in professional football and baseball, there is not one—count 'em, not one—single canine mascot? Sure, there's lions and tigers and bears (oh my!), and some people have a fascination with fish, but not one loyal, faithful, smart canine. Geeesh! So, when Anne and Tony go out on Friday nights and make their all-day treks to Sewanee on Saturdays, I tune in the Georgia or Mississippi State game. Hey, what they don't know won't hurt them! And yes, I watch the game from the couch, but let's keep that between you and me.

One of my favorite names is Jack, Ever Hopeful. That's what Tony calls me when I sit in the kitchen watching someone cook or get something out of the fridge or cabinet or whatever. Now, I don't beg, but you know, if something should fall, well…Tony keeps telling visitors we don't have a five-second rule in our house because nothing ever actually makes it to the floor. That's a little hyperbole on his part because I do remember…let's see, I think it was Christmas two years ago, when there was some cornbread dressing falling off a spoon over by the stove and an olive popping off the vegetable tray at the same time completely on the other side of the kitchen. So, it was dressing or olive…dressing or olive…you guess which one hit the floor.

Tony claims I never met a hand I didn't want to lick, and there may be some truth to that, since I consider myself a gregarious host to all our guests. I still do the bit where I lie down and wag my tail, thumping it against the floor. I do this, of course, in the hope of a tummy rub, and it works almost every time. Certainly, it always works with Tony, who simply can't resist leaning down for, if nothing else, a couple of good rubs. It's the tail that gets them. I know because Tony calls me Tailwagger Jack a lot. He also calls me Bubba a lot. Now, when *he* does it, I answer because he's my best friend, but when somebody else does it, I generally ignore them—unless, of course, I think I can get either a treat or a tummy rub out of it.

So, it's been eleven Christmases now, and in those years, I have been given a number of names: Jack, the Christmas Dog, Jingle Dog, Whoosh Dog, Scooch Dog, Adventure Dog,

Alarm Dog, Ever Hopeful, and the old standby—Tailwagger Jack. But the one I like best is the one Tony uses when he moves my bed closer to his every night and says, "Good night, Jack, Best Dog Ever." Yep, that's my favorite.

But hey, it's Christmas Eve, and I have to get up and go to the hallway and be Jack the Jingle Dog for the grandkids, and then tomorrow, I get to be Jack the Christmas Dog all over again.

A Poor Christmas

"I WANT A NEW BIKE. My old one is…" He thinks a moment and then emphatically declares, "*OLD!*" It seems to him enough of an explanation.

"And I want a new Xbox. All the kids at school are getting the new Xbox for Christmas. If I don't get one too, they'll make fun of me."

The boy is seven, perhaps eight. He does not sit on Santa's lap; rather, he stands next to Santa's large, throne-like chair. Santa no longer takes children onto his lap because the mall is afraid of being sued over possible accusations of child sexual abuse. In fact, Santa does not touch the children. His elf assistant invites the child to stand next to Santa, and if the child is too small, a parent is required to hold the child. Once the child informs Santa of his name and what she or he wants for Christmas, the requisite photo is taken, and the parent is handed the claim number for paying and picking up copies of the photo at the nearby kiosk. Then the next child is ushered in by Santa's elf.

"Why do you think they'll make fun of you if you don't get a new Xbox?" Santa takes a chance. He is writing a book about being a mall Santa, and this is his third year of research.

"Because I'm poor. They always make fun of me because I'm poor."

"Are there other poor children at your school?" Santa is interested.

"I don't know. I suppose so. It doesn't matter, though, because *I'm poor.*" He whines the answer. "That's what my old man says. He says people treat us different because *we're poor.*" Again, he whines it.

"Is your father here today?" Santa is interested.

"Yeah, that's him over there." The boy points to a man standing behind the ropes who's talking on a cell phone.

Santa can assess this father in one glance. He's wearing a short-sleeved T-shirt even though the temperature outside is in the forties. His muscular arms bear brightly colored tattoos running from his wrists up through his shirt-sleeves, out his shirt collar, and up onto his neck. The tattoos are flame-like patterns. The rest of the father's outfit includes the requisite jeans and heavy work boots. His hair is buzzed close to his scalp. He has an air of impatience about him. He is agitated about something.

"And is this your mother?" Santa asks, nodding toward a dull-eyed pregnant woman standing just out of touching range.

"Yeah, that's the old lady." The boy is dismissive, almost derisive in his tone.

"She's knocked up. I'm going to have a baby brother." He says this in a tone that indicates he obviously doesn't want a baby brother, which he then confirms. "I don't want a brother, and the old lady said she didn't want to be knocked up, but my old man says we'll get more money from the government if we have another kid."

"He does, does he?" This isn't the first time Santa has heard this one.

"What kind of work does your father do?" Santa asks.

"He doesn't work. He can't. He's disabled." The boy answers in what sounds a rehearsed response.

"He is, is he?" Santa tries not to sound incredulous as he once again notices the man's muscular physique of which he is obviously proud. Hence the tight T-shirt in forty-degree weather. Santa does, however, notice the wife is carrying two coats and wearing her own. He need not guess the relationship of husband to wife in this marriage. Experience has proven him right more often than not. Why else would the woman have the hollow, long-seeing eyes of an inmate serving a life sentence?

His original plan for the book had been to collect and relate poignant and funny stories about children at Christmas with Santa, and, in fact, he had a few such stories. It was amazing how children could blurt out the funniest things in response to Santa's questions. But, on the whole, this book was shaping up to be an indictment of the secular Christmas and the learned sense of entitlement it had brought today's youth. Very few of the people he met at the mall understood that Santa had started life as St. Nicholas and that Santa Claus was simply a phonetic transliteration of the Dutch *Sinterklaas*, which itself was a phonetically corrupted transliteration of the Greek for St. Nicholas. Perhaps, he thought, there could be no religion in Santa Claus, or the mall would be sued twelve ways from Sunday.

"Well, have you been good?" Originally the question had been followed by, "You know Santa only brings toys to boys and girls who have been good." But the last sentence had to be dropped because of complaints to mall management that parents believed Santa was accusing their child of not having been good.

"Yeah, sure. I've been good."

"Well then, I'm sure you'll get what you deserve." Santa really can't take much more of this boy. "Smile for the camera."

"Aw, we don't want no pictures, unless they're free. The old man says we can't afford no pictures unless you'll take food stamps for them."

"Well, no. I'm afraid we don't take food stamps." Santa has also heard this one.

"Well, you should. My old man says they're as good as money. He says the jerks that work in the stores will take them for anything. He gets his smokes with stamps and—"

Before he can go further, the boy's mother grabs his arm and, on the edge of violently, yanks him toward the exit of Santa's workshop.

"How many times have we told you not to talk about the food stamps?" She is more than a little agitated. She turns back to Santa. "You shouldn't ask him personal questions like that. I have half a mind to report you to the manager."

Two years ago, such a threat would have very much worried Santa, but the mall had installed a camera to record all of Santa's good little girls and boys, as well as their parents, and Santa is now wired with microphones, one from the mall and one for his own research. So, no, he isn't worried about her reporting him.

The next two in line are small children whose mothers want pictures with Santa. When each mother attempts to place her child in Santa's lap, Santa's elf blocks the path, explaining Santa does not hold children. The first mother stands next to Santa, holding her little girl, and the photo is taken. The second declines to stay when the elf explains and leaves the workshop mumbling loudly about standing in line for so long and then Santa won't even take a picture with her son. She may well complain to management, but again, Santa doesn't care. Santa isn't caring about a lot at the moment. His cynicism level for all things Christmas has been reached and may well overflow. It does almost every day around this time.

A few more children make their way through the line. They want the usual electronic games, in-line skates, bicycles, and such. Santa is looking forward to his break. He turns to his right to look at the clock above the exit to the workshop. Five more minutes.

When he turns back, she's standing there. A small, dark-eyed girl in a too-small fluffy pink coat and cap, her mother's hands lightly on her shoulders. Both mother and child have deep-set eyes that seem to express lives of pain. Both have pallid cheeks. The little girl reaches out to him with pale hands. Santa sees the bruises on her wrists and forearms as the too-small coat pulls up her arms. He fights the urge to reach down and take her in his arms.

As he leans back, she asks, "Santa?" He cannot pick her up; he cannot save her. He is angry. Can he report the abuse? It must be abuse. Looking at the mother's pained face, he thinks perhaps she too may be the victim of abuse.

He tries to talk to the girl. "What's your name?"

"Angie," she says, her arms still appealing for him to lift her onto his lap.

"Angie is a pretty name. What do you want for Christmas, Angie?"

"I want my Mommy to stop crying." Her answer catches him unprepared.

The mother leans forward, still holding Angie's shoulders. She whispers to Santa, "You're the closest Santa to the hospital. She's talked of nothing else for days." Then, in a voice that Santa has to strain to hear, she adds, "She has leukemia."

Without conscious thought, he lifts the child. She weighs nothing. She sits in his lap, her face against the red polyester of his suit. She almost burrows, seeking the warmth and protection the myth offers. She sighs.

Tears form in her mother's eyes, but Santa reaches out with his left hand and places it on top of her hand. "No more tears, please. It's her Christmas wish." The mother fights them back as she watches her child held in the arms of Santa Claus.

He motions for the elf to close the line and the doors to Santa's workshop. He tells Angie, "Your mother has stopped crying; see, she's laughing now." Her mother tries hard to laugh. She manages a smile at the contentment on Angie's face.

"You promise you will come to see me Christmas Eve?" The child's voice is more question than statement.

"Yes, I promise," Santa says. "I promise." He promises only because somewhere in his heart, he knows Santa will not forget her.

And now a smiling Angie crawls down from his lap and takes her mother's hand. "See, Mommy, I told you Santa could help." She gently pulls her mother toward the exit, turning momentarily to wave at Santa over her shoulder. He waves back.

Santa does not work the next shift. He has violated the company's policy. He reports himself. His elf is sad to see him go. She thinks he was the by far the best of the mall's Santas.

Two weeks before Christmas, and he has no job, but now he has his book. Now he has captured the magic, and each night he prays for Angie. He is not a religious man although he was raised in the church. His college classmates and professors convinced him that God was simply a crutch for those who could not truly understand. God is, they said, a myth that, once explained rationally, evaporates. He isn't sure he does understand, but he doesn't want others to think he doesn't, so God and Santa have to go. But now, he prays. Each night he gets on his knees and prays to God for the life and soul of Angie. He writes in the book how she has energized anew his faith in the old myths that explained so much about the world and God. How she has given him back Christmas. He does not, however, mention his praying.

The next October, when the sales of his book take off, he attends many book signings and answers many questions. In Chicago, a woman asks, "Do you think of it as divine intervention? Isn't Angie short for Angela?"

He compliments her perceptiveness, and that night, as he prays, he thanks God once again for sending such a small, beautiful angel to restore his faith.

A December Rain

THE SKY WAS QUICKLY CLOUDING up as he pedaled homeward. He wondered if tomorrow would be a wet throw. He might get lucky, though, and have it blow through today. He would watch the six o'clock weather report on TV tonight, but they hardly ever got it right.

There would be no morning paper on Christmas, so he got that day off, as well as New Year's Day. He pitied the poor slobs who threw the afternoon paper, because they would have to deliver on the holiday. But Christmas was still a week away, and he would have to throw every day until then.

His hands were freezing. Although it hardly ever got cold enough on the Gulf Coast for him to wear gloves, this year the weather had been more like stuff that happened up North.

His only experience with going north had been a year ago when he had accompanied his father on a business trip to New York City. The train took two full days to get there, and then he and his father had to stand outside Pennsylvania Station forever before they could catch a taxi for the hotel. He thought he would never be warm again. The restaurant that evening had seemed like heaven.

Well, heaven this morning would be the living room of his house. It was certainly cold enough for a fire in the fireplace, and he hoped his father had one going. They had used his uncle's pickup truck to bring wood all the way down from his grandfather's farm in northern Mississippi. There was hickory, oak, some poplar, and some really good-smelling cedar. A little pine also gave the room a festive smell. He liked the way it scented the room.

They had put the Christmas tree up in the corner of the living room, and its smell had begun to creep through to the dining room and hallway. With a stick or two of pine on the fire, very nice! All in all, it was turning into an OK holiday season. His brother and sister were doing their best to help out, so with a little luck, they'd have a nice Christmas. He wasn't sure why, but he had a feeling this needed to be a good holiday. It was one of the "feelings" that came on him from time to time. He didn't know why, and often didn't completely understand them, but he somehow knew that this thing or that thing needed to happen. Sometimes he could make it so, sometimes he couldn't.

He had spoken with his father about it. His father called it intuition and explained that some people were either gifted or cursed—depending upon how they dealt with the situation—with what some called a second sight. It didn't happen all that often, but there had been moments before when he had felt a strong sense that this or that needed to happen—and today it was a shapeless sensation that this Christmas needed to be a nice one.

As he passed the house, he could see they were going to need some paint on the side in the spring. The two-story house stretched out over the entire lot, its front just a few feet off the sidewalk and its back just a couple of yards from the back of the double-sized corner lot. Not overly large, it was still the biggest house on the street, and the two-car garage made it even more impressive in a middle-class sort of way.

The magnolia leaves had lost their luster in the overcast gloom that was no longer night but not yet day. The fig and pear trees stood bare, their branches like skeletal fingers reaching upward toward the lowering clouds.

As he rounded the corner and swung down into his one-foot-on-the-pedal, other-foot-in-space coasting position, he had to alter his normal route into the driveway because of Uncle Charlie's Cadillac. It loomed up out of the semidarkness like a cargo ship out of the fog on the bay. It was awfully early for Uncle Charlie to be at the house.

He parked his bike in the garage, going quickly to the sink along the wall to run some hot water over his hands. Toweling off, he loped up the back steps through the mud-room, making sure to wipe his tennis shoes. He had a little trouble getting out of his coat because he had grown a size or two and the coat had not. Hanging it on the peg, above which was stenciled "J.B.," he stepped through the vestibule and into the large kitchen, which took up much of the back of the house. The warmth welcomed him like an old friend.

And his old friend, Manfred the Wonder Dog, welcomed him like...well, like an old friend.

Kneeling to scratch Manfred behind the ears, he took in the tableau of a normal Saturday morning in his house. His mother was at the stove using a spatula to push some bacon grease up over the frying eggs. On the back of the stove was a pot of rice. The oven gave off the smell of biscuits almost done, and on the sideboard laid a platter with a pound or so of just-fried bacon. Off at the counter across the room and to his right, his sister was grinding oranges on the juicer, and his brother was taking pear and fig preserves out of the refrigerator and putting them on the lazy Susan in the middle of the large table that separated him from his mother. And overlying all the smells was the odor of fresh-brewed, very strong coffee with chicory. If only he could bottle the smells of that morning, he would make a million dollars. When you're thirteen, a million dollars is about as much money as there is in the world.

"Any problems with the route?" his mother asked.

"No, ma'am. Just that dog that crazy wrestler has over on Leadyard Street. I swear he's going to get loose one day and tear my leg off."

"Well, do you want your father to go over there and speak to him?"

"No, ma'am. I guess if I can't get close enough to collect what he owes, I just won't throw him a paper, and he can ask to borrow his neighbor's or something."

"I'd call the police," his older brother, P.J., chimed in.

"And tell them what? I'm afraid of his dog? Can't go doing that. I bet every one of the guys with a route has at least one dog to deal with. Didn't you have a dog to mess with on your route?"

"What's that guy's name anyway?" his brother asked. "Chief Thunderstick, right?"

"No, his real name—or at least the name on the subscription—is John Tolliver. He claims to be an Apache Indian, and the name they call him in the ring is Chief Strong Wind. All I know is he has a big German shepherd, and when I go by there to collect, he sometimes threatens to sic the dog on me. So, last Friday evening, when I go to collect for like two months he hasn't paid, you know what he says? 'I didn't subscribe to get the paper.' He tells me I've been throwing his paper for over a year, and he didn't subscribe! So, I show him the subscription notebook. He looks at it and tells me that's not him."

"Not him? What's that supposed to mean?" his mother asked.

"That's what I said. So, he tells me his name isn't John Tolliver, it's John Tallifferreo. T-a-l-l-i-f-f-e-r-r-e-o," J.B. said, spelling out the Italian version of the name.

"He says his name is spelled wrong, and it's not his fault if the newspaper got it wrong. He says he doesn't owe anything because the name is some other guy's name. And he's no more an Apache Indian than I am. His cousin is in the ninth grade over at Mae Eanes Junior High. He plays on the football team.

"I mean, I not only lose my two cents on the paper I throw him, but I also have to make up the thirteen cents the company gets for the paper. So, every week I'm going more than a dollar in the hole just giving him a paper. Right now, he owes me eight dollars and twenty cents. That's a lot of money. I'm not collecting again until next Friday, so if I don't throw him a paper, I should get his attention by then."

"Well, in a way, he's right," J.B.'s brother said, reaching back into the refrigerator for the big bowl of butter on the bottom shelf. "You know how much you hate it when somebody around here sends us something with 'Jordan' as our last name, or when somebody calls you 'Gene.' It's the English inability to recognize the different sounds in our names and so they just go with the most common. There are, after all, a lot more 'Jordans' and 'Genes' in Mobile than there are 'Jourdains' and 'Jeans.'"

"OK, say that's true. It still doesn't mean this guy doesn't have to pay his bill." J.B. stood up and, reaching for the bacon platter, broke a piece in half, took a bite, and placed the rest between his lips.

"Manfred," he mumbled, holding the bacon between his lips and bending down to the sitting dog.

Manfred reached upward with his mouth and gently took the bacon from J.B.'s lips.

"Jean Baptiste!" His mother's raised voice was more the beginning of a laugh than a true scolding. "Stop that, or we won't have enough bacon for breakfast. Your uncle Charlie is here."

Actually, Uncle Charlie was just his uncle by marriage. He was married to J.B.'s father's sister—Aunt Isabelle. If Charlie had been his father's real brother, he would have a French name like everyone else in the family.

J.B. walked over to the sink to rinse the bacon grease off his fingers. While standing there, with the warm water further restoring blood flow to his red, chapped hands, he thought about his family. His real uncles were named Louis, Remy, and Etienne. They were his father's brothers. His father was Honoré Baptiste, and his brother was Pierre Jouet. His sister was Margaux Emmanuelle, known to her school friends as Margie, and to her family as "Me"—as in the pronoun.

His mother was Francoise, and all together they were the Jourdains. A family as old as Mobile. J.B.'s great-great-great-etc.-grandfather had been a soldier with the Sieur de Bienville, and had married one of the cassette girls brought to Mobile by the French government.

Now they were all anglicized, except, of course, their names. All the men were called by their initials—H.B., P.J., and J.B. Their mother was the only one who used her actual name. So, she was Francoise to her friends, and Mrs. Honoré Jourdain to strangers or casual acquaintances.

Me was home from the university for Christmas break. She was some kind of prodigy, J.B. explained to his friends. She was nineteen, but she had almost finished her bachelor's degree and was already taking courses for a master's. She was a whiz-bang mathematician like her father.

P.J. was in his senior year at McGill High School. He was only seventeen, but he would be going to college next year, probably at Springhill, since the baseball coach there salivated every time P.J. was in the room. The Dodgers had already sent an agent to talk to him about signing a contract, but P.J. knew too many people who had thrown out their arms, or gotten hurt, or been drafted into the army to think about signing a professional contract right out of high school. He believed his future was in business, like his father.

J.B. was just J.B. He was thirteen and in the eighth grade. His grades were good—mostly *A*s with an occasional *B* sprinkled here and there. He didn't, however, show the proclivity for math his sister had, or the quick uptake and processing skills P.J. evidenced. He loved to read, and he retained information like a sponge. He was always coming up with bits and pieces of trivial information about this and that. His father called him "a veritable cornucopia of useless information." His mother was always telling him that he was more like her and her family—good, solid, practical, commonsense farmers. Yet she had a degree in chemistry from the university and could more than hold her own in discussions on everything from math to politics. On the latter, she was more than a little opinionated.

"Father Honoré," as some of his business associates called him—mostly behind his back, because at six three and 230 pounds, it wouldn't have been wise to do it to his face—was a soft-spoken individual with the patois of the port city. He almost never raised his voice, and in fact, opponents discovered that the fainter his voice became, the more trouble they were going to get. He was a fair man who insisted upon fairness all round—which made him an unlikely person to be a director in a local group of influential businessmen who managed business, politics, sports, entertainment, and other endeavors all up and down the Gulf Coast. They were in direct competition with the members of the Boston Club in New Orleans, but the "Société," as it was known, was somewhat older, better organized, and in closer contact with the working-class levels of the region.

On paper, Honoré owned four taxi companies (a monopoly in Mobile County), three nightclub restaurants (including the very popular Café Royale), the majority of shares in four banks, and part of the local double-A baseball team. He was as legitimate as you could be, and still be successful in a world where money, name, and patronage were how you made it.

The nickname "Father" had followed him from his days at Springhill College, where it had been generally assumed that he would become either a brother or a Jesuit priest and a professor of mathematics. That he had not done so surprised more than a few of his classmates and, indeed, most of the professors at the college. Apparently, discovering women had been his downfall.

The warm water flowing over J.B.'s hands was so soothing, he would have stood there mentally climbing his family tree for several more minutes except his sister pushed him aside, using her hips while holding her hands like a doctor washing up.

"Hey, squirt, move over. I need to wash this sticky juice off my hands."

He pushed back with his hips, and a battle of position began. Six years younger, he was still bigger than his sister, who, at five eight, was pretty tall for a girl. He was winning the battle until his father walked in and observed what was happening. He put his hands under J.B.'s armpits and almost casually lifted him to the side, dropped him unceremoniously, then reached over for dish towel, which he dropped over J.B.'s head.

"Dry your hands and leave your sister alone."

"Where's Charlie?" his wife asked.

"Gone to the Seaman's Hall for breakfast. They want him to take a ship down to Panama for somebody. Then he'll catch the next boat headed this way through the canal."

Uncle Charlie was a shipmaster and sailed all over the world on cargo ships. Sometimes Aunt Isabelle went with him, but mostly she didn't. Charlie was gone sometimes for two months when he made a trip to Asia. Lately he had been serving as a harbor pilot for Mobile Harbor, but he still took the occasional voyage as well.

"So, what was so important, he had to talk to you at seven o'clock on a Saturday morning?" she asked.

"What do you think?" He poured coffee from the pot into the restaurant-style cup.

"Louis?"

"Exactly. Belle wants to go with Charlie on the trip to Panama, but she's concerned about what to do with Louis. Charlie wondered if we could take him for a month or so."

"Well, I guess we could do it, although asking Dora to take on the responsibility during the day is, I think, a little too much."

"I know. Dora's a great maid, but I think she would worry too much about Louis and not get her other chores done."

"We could hire somebody," his wife mused.

"Sure we could, but without some time for them to get acquainted with Louis first, I'm not sure that's the best idea. Maybe I could take Louis to the office with me. Maybe that would be the best idea. He's really no trouble as long as you don't let him wander off when he's having one of his moments."

"I suppose they want to have Christmas in Panama," Francoise said.

"Yes, that's the reason Charlie was over here early. They want him to take the ship out day after tomorrow. It's an old Liberty ship like he skippered during the war, so he'll have no problems knowing the systems and such."

H.B. sat at the table and gently tilted the hot cup so that coffee flowed over the rim and into his saucer. He placed the cup on his plate and, taking the saucer with two hands, raised it to his lips and blew gently to cool the liquid. Then he sipped at it.

"I told him I'd pick Louis up later today." He sipped again. "You know, this whole thing could be a lot worse. What if Louis was blind or a double amputee like so many of the other guys who came home injured? What if he was bedridden and had to live in a VA home? It's been what, fourteen years since the war? And he's done OK."

"He's done OK because you help him all the time," his wife answered. "You know it's your duty as the oldest, and I know it, and Belle knows it, but I'm not so sure about Remy or Etienne." Francoise lifted the fried eggs one at a time and slid them onto a large platter. She turned to place the platter on the table and faced H.B. "I love your family dearly, but sometimes I wonder if they all depend too much on you."

It was true, J.B. thought. There did seem to be a lot of problems his father had to sort out for his brothers and sister. His grandparents were dead, and his father had taken over as head of the family.

His father sipped his coffee and then, looking up over the saucer, said, "Well, they do some, but that's what being the oldest sibling in a family is all about—and dear, that's what I do for a living. I solve problems."

"Dad?" J.B. asked. "Have you heard from the navy about Uncle Louis's veteran's benefits? I thought you said they might pay him enough to hire someone to live with him full time so he didn't have to stay at Aunt Belle's."

"No, J.B. We haven't heard anything other than they can't find some parts of his record. Particularly the period from when he was in the hospital at Pearl Harbor until he was evacuated from Iwo Jima."

J.B.'s uncle Louis had been a marine corps lieutenant in World War II and had come home suffering from the effects of having been wounded at Guadalcanal and then again at Iwo Jima. Something had happened to him, and he had what J.B.'s father referred to as "spells," where he regressed into some place and time in 1943 or '44. He wasn't violent or anything; he just had conversations with people who weren't really there. Still, he could wander off looking for people or places, and since he thought he was in Hawaii or on a ship or someplace like that, he might get run over or fall or something. People didn't know how to handle it when he fell into one of the spells, and mostly they just tried to avoid him.

When he wasn't having a spell, he was—for the most part—a sad person, because he knew full well about his spells and that he couldn't hold a job. He also knew he couldn't get married or have a family, and that made him even sadder. His spells lasted from ten or fifteen minutes to three or four days. The only people who seemed to truly understand his situation were J.B.'s father and Aunt Belle, who was Uncle Louis's fraternal twin.

J.B. still didn't understand how a woman could be a fraternal twin, because his Latin (he was in his third year) made it clear "fraternal" meant brother. Still, he guessed he understood that it really meant "not identical."

He sat in his chair at the table and crossed himself as his father began, *"In nomine Patris et Filii..."*

After grace, everyone passed the platters around the table or spun the lazy Susan to get the butter, jam, or preserves. There was nothing better than a fried egg on top of a big spoonful of sticky rice and some crisp, thick bacon or salt pork. Biscuits with butter, pear, or homemade fig preserves, and some milk or hot coffee—it was the breakfast of champions. At least it was in the Deep South, and in December 1959, you couldn't get any farther south (metaphorically) than Mobile, Alabama.

After the initial silence that falls on all tables supplied with good food, H.B. asked, "Did I hear somebody wouldn't pay his bill for your newspaper services?"

J.B. re-explained the problem with his wrestler. His father nodded and said he thought J.B.'s plan not to throw the newspaper was a good alternative. "Let him think about it awhile. He'll come around," was all he said.

As they began to leave the table, J.B. asked, "Say, Dad, you don't suppose Uncle Louis is having the same problem we are, do you?"

"In what way, 'the same problem,' J.B.?"

"Well, I mean, maybe his records are in somebody's file whose name is Jordan or Gordon. You know how they do it. Or maybe he's got a separate file with his name spelled wrong, kind of like l-e-w-i-s for l-o-u-i-s?"

"You may have something there, J.B. Although the files are supposed to be by service number, I wonder if there could be two or more files with the same service number. I've been corresponding with the St. Louis file center so much, I have a telephone number for one of the supervisors. I'll call him long distance first thing Monday and ask." He put his cup down and pushed away from the table.

"So how about you come with me to get your uncle Louis? I know he'll be happy to see you."

"Dad, actually, I see Uncle Louis almost every morning. He's always up and sitting on Aunt Belle's porch when I throw the paper. The mornings he's not there, I always think he must be having one of his spells. Otherwise, I always wave and yell out, 'Morning, Uncle Louis.' Sometimes I stop a minute to talk. He seems to like it if I do. I think he likes the early-morning smell of the bakery down the street. I always mean to go back by and offer to take him to the bakery restaurant, but I either have to get to school or, like today, the rain seemed ready to set in. But maybe we can go a little later and stop by the bakery for a doughnut and some milk."

"Sure," his father said. "We can do that. How about we go over about ten or so?"

J.B. went out to the garage, turned the space heater on, and began to stitch up the latest hole in one of his three newspaper bags. Then he oiled his bike and made sure he had his oilskins ready to go. He had bought a set of rain gear at the seaman's supply down near the shipyard. They would keep him dry enough, but his big problem was the papers. He pulled out the oilskin poncho he used to shelter the papers while they were in the bags on his handlebars. He would have to make sure each paper wound up on the porch in a dry spot, or he would have to get off his bike and put the paper behind the screen door for the houses that didn't have porches. It would take him much longer to throw his route tomorrow, especially since it was Sunday and the papers would be much larger. Then he went inside and began sorting out how much each subscriber owed him, and projected what he expected to collect next Friday afternoon.

By ten o'clock, he had his accounts figured out and had begun to work on the paper his social studies teacher had assigned his class to have in just after New Year's: "Why War Isn't the Answer." He knew what she wanted, but he wasn't sure how to write a paper about it.

In the full light of day, the sky looked even more ominous than it had in the gray gloom of dawn. The clouds were low and dark gray, but it had not yet begun to rain. He suspected this would be one of those occasions when it drizzled more than it poured. He wasn't sure why, but the feeling he got was that this was more than a passing storm or front. This was a system settling in. He hoped he was wrong, but somehow he always seemed to be right about the weather. Something the sailors down at Seaman's Hall called "having a weather eye." It was like his other "feelings." He just seemed to know.

On the way to his aunt's house, which wasn't all that far, he asked his father, "Dad, this really isn't about money, is it? I mean, I know you have enough money to let Uncle Louis live independently, and I know you would give it to him. So why do we have to go to the trouble of trying to find his military records?"

His father thought for a moment and then pulled the car to the curb and put it in park.

"You're right, J.B. It isn't about money. So, if it isn't money, what do you think it's about?"

"Well…" J.B. turned to face his father and leaned against the passenger door. "I think Uncle Louis doesn't want people to take care of him, but it isn't really about now—it's about something before. When I look into his eyes, I see someone whose soul is wounded. Not his body and not his mind. He wants very badly to be whole, and he can't seem to find the way to make that happen. I don't think the money will make him happier, but I think it will make him feel less a burden to others. There's something else there, but what it is just seems to slip out of my hands as I try to capture it."

H.B. considered his son a moment and then quietly said, "J.B., I think there yet may be a real 'Father' in the family."

He put the car in gear, and they continued on.

In the dimness of the day, his uncle Louis seemed even sadder. He almost never smiled, even when J.B. made one of his excellent wordplays. It was a game J.B. and his father played. Puns and corny jokes. Groans were often more appreciated than actual laughs.

At the bakery shop, H.B. ordered six glazed doughnuts and three cups of coffee. They sat in a booth along the wall of the long, narrow room. The smell of fresh bread suffused the room as it always did. Mingled with it were undertones of fresh coffee and that wonderful aromatic scent sugared icing brings to the mix. It was a place that never failed to lift J.B.'s spirits, and yet Uncle Louis seemed determined to remain a dispirited lump. This, for J.B., had become a personal challenge.

"So, Uncle Louis, why is six afraid of seven?"

"What?" his uncle asked.

"Why is six afraid of seven?" J.B. repeated.

"I don't know. Why is six afraid of seven?"

"Because seven ate nine." J.B. chuckled, his father smirked, and Uncle Louis just sat there.

Seated across from his uncle, J.B. was not to be denied. "And speaking of eight, is it true that you can divide it in half, square the two halves, and end up with nothing?"

His uncle looked quizzical but only for a moment.

"If you mean you take the zero top half of the figure eight and the zero bottom half and square either or both to arrive at a final answer of zero, then the answer is yes."

"Oh, you've heard it," J.B. deadpanned, then looked sideways at his father. "Dad, are you stealing my jokes again?"

"Steal them? Why on earth would I steal them? I have plenty of my own bad jokes!"

The interplay drew the briefest and slightest of grins from Louis.

"Aha!" J.B. shouted and pointed at his uncle. "I saw it. He grinned." Leaning over and looking earnestly in his uncle's eyes, he continued. "Now see here, Uncle Louis. If you're going to spend Christmas with us, we don't allow anybody to feel sad over Christmas. It's a rule in the house that even if you don't feel happy, you have to pretend. Right, Dad?"

His father looked only a little taken aback by J.B.'s forthrightness but quickly recovered and supported his son. "Absolutely. House rules. Everybody acts happy during Christmas."

"So, Uncle Looouie." J.B. dragged the name out a full second. "I'm going to loan you a joke book, and every day you're going to tell at least two, count 'em, two jokes while we're in a family situation. Right, Dad?"

"Oh yes, absolutely. Two, no less!" His father was getting into the spirit.

"Yes, two jokes. You will have practiced them so that your delivery is good, and you will not read them. Two jokes a day. You must obtain a laugh or at least a decent groan. If you need help, I'll be there. I suggest you not ask your older brother, because he can't tell a joke without sniggling before he gets to the punch line."

"What do you mean, sniggling? Why, I'll have you know I have them rolling on the floor in the office."

"Wouldn't have a thing to do with you being the boss, would it?"

The bantering continued, and it seemed that what made Louis smile the most wasn't the jokes, good or bad, but the spirited battle between father and youngest son, each striving to topple the other from his perceived acme of humor. And realizing this, father and son played it to the hilt so that by the time they returned home, Louis, while not Mr. Enthusiasm, wasn't Mr. Let-Me-Wallow-in-My-Depression either.

Dinner was followed by an evening in front of the fireplace, with H.B. telling stories about Louis as a child, helping them bond as a family settling in to celebrate Christmas.

The next morning the mist started a little after three. By four thirty, it had developed into a steady drizzle and, as J.B. had prophesied, looked as if it was there to stay a while. It was wet, and it was cold. This, unfortunately, was winter in Mobile. Forty degrees and 100 percent humidity—or as close to that as you can get when it's raining. The night air was so heavy with moisture, J.B. almost felt resistance as he pedaled out of the garage.

The boys rolled into the substation pretty much on time. Somebody had lit a fire in an old fifty-gallon drum, and while they'd have liked to stand by the drum to get warm, it was just outside the overhang and to get near, they had to stand in the drizzle. Those with appropriate rain gear didn't mind. They stood close by the drum, letting the drizzle trickle down their oilskin helmets and into the mud, which had been stirred to a gummy consistency by their rubber deck boots. Those with skimpier rain hats and coats, or with no rubber boots, would turn their collars up, hunch in the rain for a few moments near the drum, and then scamper back to the open-sided shelter.

The distributor finally arrived in the delivery truck and began tossing the bundles of papers onto the concrete floor of the shelter. J.B. had to find his bundles—those that said "Route SE-5"—cut the wires that held the bundles together, and then fold each paper. But since these were Sunday papers, he had to roll each one, put a rubber band around the paper, and then stand it upright in his delivery bag. He had to buy the rubber bands, so he guessed that on Sundays, he made less than two cents a paper—but you couldn't lease a route for just Monday through Saturday.

Once he had all the papers rolled up and stowed, he had filled two bags and part of the third. He placed the first bag on the front of his bike, the strap up and over his upturned handlebars. He set the second bag securely into the top of the first and hung the strap of the third around his neck with the bag resting on the crossbar of his bike. He put the poncho over the two bags on his handlebars, with the tail tucked in over the third bag and against his chest. The head flap on the poncho was over the second bag, allowing access to the papers while still protecting them from most of the rain.

He pushed off, standing to pedal to get the heavy load under way, then settled back onto his seat, keeping a steady pace for the two miles he had to cover to reach his route. The rain stung his face, but that didn't last long, because the cold was making it numb. By the time he had gone a mile, his nose had begun to run, and he wiped at it with the left sleeve of his raincoat.

He reached the entry point to his route and began to carefully wind his way in and out of the driveways and sidewalks, ensuring every throw made cover. The last thing he wanted was to have to stop, try to steady his bike in an upright position, and recover a misthrown paper. He thought about just throwing another paper from his bag since he usually had about six extras and didn't think he would make that many errors. Still, he would lose money if he did, and he wasn't about losing money.

One nice thing about a cold rain was that the dogs were under cover and didn't like coming out any more than J.B. liked being out. Toward the end of his route, he passed Aunt Belle's house, which looked dark since Uncle Louis wasn't on the porch waiting for the paper. He'd have to remember not to throw them a paper while they were gone to Panama.

When he was done, he knew every paper—all hundred and fifty of them—had reached a covered spot, even though he had almost turned the bike over three or four times while straddling the crossbar as he stopped and reached to open a screen door to place the paper. Still, he was sure somebody would call the paper and tell them he or she had received a wet paper that morning. He would find out about it at the brief meeting on Monday morning at the substation.

As he exited his route, he could smell the bakery. In the drizzle, the aroma was even sweeter than usual, and the air just a little warmer. Nothing would have pleased him more than to slide into a booth and order some hot doughnuts and coffee, but he was on his way to St. Matthews for the eight o'clock Mass. He was the acolyte for Father Sheen, so he needed to get there, change out of his rain gear and into a cassock and cotta, and then check to ensure the cruets, the lavabo, the towels, and all the other things associated with Communion had been placed correctly by the altar guild. They always were, but it was his job to check.

There were few people at the eight o'clock Mass because of the rain. Ordinarily there would have been forty or fifty people wanting to get their required Mass done and get on to other Sunday chores, but this morning there were barely twenty.

Done with the Mass, he pedaled home. The rain was heavier but still not a downpour. It smacked his oilskin helmet enough to sound like woodpeckers working on a dead tree, and it was still very cold. Taking off his rain gear in the garage, he made sure the space heater was on so that his gear would dry and be warm when he had to put it on again. He knew the rain was here for a while and anticipated that at least Monday and Tuesday would be wet throws.

The house was empty save for Manfred the Wonder Dog, who greeted him as a hero returned from a long absence. His mother had left a covered plate on the sideboard with some cold bacon and biscuits. He turned the gas on under the coffeepot and waited for it to warm. Meanwhile, he stuffed some bacon in a biscuit and grabbed some pear preserves out of the refrigerator. When the coffee was hot, he poured a cup and sat down to read the paper he had brought in with him. Manfred sat with his head on J.B.'s knee, accepting the occasional bite of bacon as rings from the king to a thane.

Finishing the paper (there was little of interest), J.B. decided to try to work on his school assignment. He sat at his desk, sharpening his pencil, arranging his notebook, and writing the assignment topic at the front of the notebook. He did everything but start on the assignment. He got no further than he had gotten previously. He thought he knew what the teacher wanted, but he wasn't sure how to write it.

By one o'clock, his family was home and there was work to be done in the kitchen for Sunday dinner. Today they were having red snapper, rice, sweet-and-sour onion relish, winter squash, some fresh rolls from the bakery, and for dessert, blackberry-and-apple-pie with some of the blackberries his mom had put up this summer.

After dinner, they adjourned to the living room, where Me played the piano. She was as good on the piano as she was at extrapolating logarithms. The room was large, but the smell of the Christmas tree was everywhere. The fireplace was across the room from the piano, and they all sat with their backs to the music and their faces to the fire. H.B. went over to the piano and began to sing as Me played. He had a wonderful baritone voice, and his accent was perfect for the music. He sang "Ave Maria" beautifully.

J.B. had more appreciation for the music than would the typical thirteen-year-old. He struggled every Wednesday afternoon to master the keys but never hoped to be as good as Me or H.B. Something about math skills and music. His mother had a lovely voice but seldom sang unless she was in a group. P.J. played the guitar as well as the piano, but he too was not in the same class as his father and sister.

After the song, H.B. went upstairs and came down with a small but long case. He set it on the piano and opened it. It was a King silver clarinet. He played clarinet himself, but once he put the bell on this instrument, he took a new reed from a packet, put it on the mouthpiece, and handed the clarinet to Louis, who at first refused it, but after the right entreaties from everyone, took it and stuck the mouthpiece in his mouth to wet the reed. After a minute or so, he blew a major scale, then a chromatic one. H.B. sat down at the piano and played the first four bars of "Stardust." He looked at Louis and started again, and this time a full-toned, throaty clarinet captured the melody and sent it wafting into the ether of time, warping the continuum—and it was 1938.

Louis watched his brother as he played. He did not close his eyes to remember the tune, but seemed rather to watch the music from the bell of his metal clarinet as it floated toward the ceiling and into the invisible beyond. When he held the last note before sending it off to follow the others, there was a tear in his eye. That was quickly dried, though, and followed by sweat when H.B. launched into "St. James Infirmary" and Louis was doing runs up and down the keys. Louis was skilled and, even if out of practice, a remarkable clarinet player. At the end, he was out of breath but seemed livelier than J.B. could remember seeing him in...well, forever. He was like a really cool person.

On Monday morning, J.B. once again had a wet throw. Not much different from Sunday, but the papers were smaller. They occupied only a bag and a half.

Monday afternoon J.B. went Christmas shopping, hitting all the stores in downtown Mobile. He used an umbrella instead of his rain helmet, but he wore his deck boots because Mobile floods with only a minimal amount of rain, and while this was only a drizzle, there were still fairly deep places along the curbs and intersections where his normal loafers or tennis shoes would have become waterlogged. He kept the rain helmet in the bag he carried because he had to wear it when traveling to and from home. You couldn't carry an opened umbrella on a bike unless you were one of those guys in the circus riding a unicycle.

A scarf for his mother, some sheet music for Me, and a box of picks for P.J. He already had a gift for his father. It was a tin box with a picture of their house painted on it. J.B.

had traded one of his customers three months' worth of free newspapers to do it. It was a great gift, and one he knew his father would value.

One gift from each—that was the rule in the Jourdain family. Christmas wasn't some sort of extravaganza with piles of gifts under the tree beforehand and jungles of wrapping paper and ribbon afterward. Santa Claus was more like the Holy Ghost. He was the bringer of the spirit of Christmas, which was love and brotherhood. Early on, the Jourdain children learned it was more appropriate to ask Santa Claus to take care of the less fortunate, and every year they selected a group they would ask Santa to help. Then, like magic, on Christmas morning they would find a note from Santa on the tree telling them how he had arranged for the children at the Catholic orphanage to have toys this Christmas, or that he had helped the children at St. Joseph's Hospital, or that food had been sent to the group of families the children had selected. It was a fine way to celebrate Christmas, and there was no reason to ever stop believing in Santa since he worked like the Holy Ghost.

Now J.B. had to come up with a gift for his uncle. Nothing he had seen in any of the stores caught his eye. On his way home, his other gifts secured against the rain under his oilskin poncho, he passed an antiques shop on Conti Street. Well, the sign said "Antiques," but to J.B. it looked more like a junk shop than an antiques shop. It did have an awning under which he could rest his bike, so he went in. An antiques shop in a port city is not unlike an exotic pawnshop. Sailors bring in all manner of items, wanting to sell them to the owner. J.B. browsed through the store, occasionally asking the price on this or that item. There were no other customers, so he had the full attention of the shop's owner.

"Do you know what you're looking for?" the owner asked.

"Not really. I'm just browsing. I need a Christmas gift for my uncle."

"Do you have a price in mind?"

"Not really. I mean, not a piece of furniture or anything like that."

"Would you like to look at something like a dagger from the Middle East?"

"Not really. He doesn't need a dagger."

"Do you know what he needs?"

"Not really. That's why I'm browsing."

The owner mentally threw up his hands and left J.B. to wander the extremely tight aisles of the store.

As he turned from one aisle into another, J.B. came face-to-face with a statute of Vishnu. He recognized it from a book his father had in his library entitled, *Hinduism, the Catholic Faith of the East*. The statue momentarily transfixed him. His mental apparatus jumped ahead, and J.B. was suddenly remembering a book he liked yet didn't like. A book that had more impact on his thought than even Dostoyevsky's *Crime and Punishment*. The book was *The Razor's Edge*, by W. Somerset Maugham. J.B. was upset with himself that he hadn't seen the parallels between not just Larry Darrell but also Gray and Sophie and his uncle Louis before. Still, he did not think his uncle was experiencing a crisis of finding meaning in life. It was something else, something that amalgamated all three character crises but displayed different symptoms.

Then J.B. knew what he wanted to get Uncle Louis.

"Have you got any old coins from India? Rather large ones, I think."

Friday, the weather continued to emulate a New England fall. It remained in the forties, and the humidity made it seem even colder. J.B. wrapped up in his too-small coat and made his collection rounds. It was two days until Christmas, and nobody wanted to part with their money—especially his subscribers who lived in the Byrd Housing Project—but grumbling, they paid their bills. As he was pedaling down Leadyard Street, the wrestler ran out of his house.

"Kid! Hey, kid! Stop!"

J.B. pulled up, putting his right foot on the curb. The wrestler came outside his chain link fence. In his hand, he held several one-dollar bills.

"Hey, kid! I need to pay my bill, but I forgot what I owe ya."

J.B., somewhat surprised, pulled his account book from his coat pocket. "Eight dollars and twenty cents," he said.

"Oh, only eight dollars?" the wrestler said.

"And twenty cents," J.B. added.

"Well, look, here's eighty fifty. You can keep the change."

J.B. reached down to his belt and punched out a quarter and a nickel from his belt coin changer.

"I'm sorry, sir, but we're not allowed to accept gratuities," he said handing the change to the man.

"Oh, right. Well, listen, kid, there's a couple more things. I mean, you know I'm only having you on about the dog. I would never let him hurt you. I mean, he's really a good family dog. Just a little too protective. And, oh yeah, the last thing. You'll see that my subscription gets entered in the right name... you know, t-a-l-l-i-f-f-e-r-r-e-o. I wouldn't want there to be any misunderstanding."

He turned to go back into his house.

J.B. pushed away from the curb, encouraged that his plan had worked so well.

As he pedaled away from the house, an enormous dark-blue Lincoln pulled out of a side street and headed back to town. The rather large man at the wheel was grinning from ear to ear. H.B. had been right. The wrestler wasn't actually a tough guy, at least not when a really tough guy asked him nicely to do something.

The day before Christmas Eve, H.B. gathered the family in the living room after dinner. If "the cat who swallowed the canary" described someone pleased with himself, then this cat had feasted on an entire aviary.

"The supervisor I spoke with on Monday called me back today. Louis, they found your records. Apparently, they were filed under 'Lewis Jordan,' just as J.B. suggested. Seems you are in for some back pay and a couple of medals. Well, actually not just any old medals: two Silver Stars for gallantry. You were promoted to captain while you were on Iwo Jima, and you should have been medically retired, not just discharged with a disability. The supervisor showed the errors to *his* supervisor, and they're going to suggest the secretary of the navy present you the medals. He read me the recommendations for the medals, and Louis, you're a real hero. I mean, really a hero. Why haven't you told us about this?"

H.B. was too excited to notice the look in Louis's eyes, but J.B. caught it as Louis tried very hard to smile. It wasn't the look of a man relieved. It was more like a man trapped in a corner of an alley with nowhere to run. A little sliver of understanding revealed itself to J.B.

By Christmas Eve, the rain had stopped, but the wind had increased, and the clouds still hugged the ground like a wife seeing her husband off to war. The family would gather for an early-afternoon meal and then again to go to midnight Mass at the basilica. In between was the final wrapping of gifts, and J.B. would make sure he took a nap. He didn't want to miss any of what would follow. After Mass, they would go to the Café Royale. In years past, a small staff of volunteers would have cooked up a breakfast feast for the family. Now it would be just *café au lait* and fresh beignets and maybe some scrambled eggs with crawfish and onions. For J.B., they always had a pot of hominy grits and lots of fresh butter. There was banana pudding, and he who found the piece of hard candy in his pudding would be awarded the first gift on Christmas morning. Thus fortified, the family would return home to eventually find their way to bed.

Theirs was not the "up at the crack of dawn" Christmas celebration of other homes, but one of "up by ten o'clock" for coffee and croissants. Then everyone dressed, and by eleven thirty or so, they were in the living room to open stockings and gifts.

The rain had returned during the early-morning hours. Once again it was a cold drizzle that made people glad of being inside, especially if they had a fireplace. Me had bitten down on the hard-raspberry candy at the Café Royale, so H.B. handed her the first gift. It was J.B.'s sheet music. Me insisted on kissing J.B., which he had only recently found the fortitude not to resist. J.B.'s scarf to his mom was the second gift, and he had to endure another kiss. Thus it went until J.B. was handed a gift that was longer and wider than it was high. Removing the gift wrap revealed only a box like the kind shirts come in but larger. Taking the top off, he found a genuine US Army Air Forces A-2 bomber jacket. When he put it on, it was just a little too large.

"So, you can wear it longer," his mother said.

"Did you notice the nameplate?" his father asked.

J.B. looked down, and sewn on the left side of the breast was an actual leather nameplate. It read, in gold letters, "J.B. Jourdain." J.B. beamed. He couldn't think of a better Christmas present. Well, maybe one, but that wasn't his father's or mother's to give.

The very next gift was J.B.'s for his father, and there was a misting of eyes when the box was passed around. No kiss from his father, but a bear hug that engulfed him and during which he could have sworn he heard a slight sigh.

The small box for Louis from J.B. was presented next.

"Uncle Louis, don't open that right now," J.B. said. "A little later, maybe after dinner."

Everyone adjourned to the kitchen to help with Christmas dinner: marlin steaks with béarnaise sauce, steamed onions and apples, cheese grits made with aged gouda, marinated artichoke hearts, and for dessert, pear tarts with sweet whiskey sauce. Everyone but J.B. drank a fine French chardonnay. J.B. had a glass of pear cider that he found overly tart but declined to criticize.

Then, after dinner, everyone gathered once again in the living room, where H.B. passed around his famous planter's punch, which even J.B. was allowed to sample.

The rain became heavier, and with the wind, it attacked the windowpanes. A shutter came loose, and J.B. and P.J. ran to the front porch to secure it. Other shutters bumped and banged as the wind tore at their moorings. It had become a stormy night.

Late in the evening, when everyone had gone off to do something else, J.B. asked his uncle to open the gift. The small box revealed the coin. It was a large—as in silver dollar–sized—bronze coin from the reign of the Mughal ruler, Akbar the Great. J.B. had bartered hard for the coin with the owner of the store, finally wearing him down with the story of how he wished to use the coin. At that, the owner had taken a chance and told J.B. he would sell him the coin for whatever money J.B. had in his pocket. Having already purchased his other Christmas gifts, J.B. had six dollars remaining in his pocket, and he thought that an excellent bargain. He didn't know how the shop owner felt. Still, there it was.

Uncle Louis took the coin from the box. It shone brightly in the light from the fireplace. J.B., knowing that he was destroying the patina of age, had boiled the coin in hot salt water and then scrubbed it clean and polished it with Brasso, so now it looked as if it had just been stamped by hammer and mold. He cared not about patina but rather about shine.

"That coin is magical," J.B. said.

"Really? Magical?" Uncle Louis held the coin between his thumb and forefinger and looked at it in the light of the fireplace.

"Magical, you say. How so? And remember, J.B., I read *The Razor's Edge*. In fact, didn't you see me reading it one morning and ask me about it?"

"Oh sure, I remember, but this coin isn't like the coin in that story. Only the character Gray thought that coin was magical. Everybody else knew it was just a coin. But this coin has honest-to-goodness magical properties. Of course, the magic only works if you believe in it. Do you believe in magic, Uncle Louis?"

"I don't think so, Jean." Louis used J.B.'s given name, and J.B. could tell Louis was drifting toward one of his spells. J.B. had to keep him in the present.

"But you do believe in God. I saw you at Mass last night. You're angry with him, but you still believe in him. Well, maybe magic is very small miracles, and God makes miracles possible. It's too complicated for me to explain, but I just know it. It's as real as anything else if you know where to look."

J.B. was on his knees between the sofa and the fireplace. Louis sat on the front edge of the sofa. J.B. leaned forward and took the coin. He held it so the light from the fireplace was reflected off the shiny bronze of the coin and onto the ceiling.

"Think about it, Uncle Louis. Someone held this coin in front of a fire five hundred years ago. Perhaps it cast its light onto a tent or maybe onto the ceiling in Akbar's palace. How did he come by the coin? Did he steal it? Beg it? Borrow it? Earn it? Did he sell his goods or produce for it? Was it a tax? Who was that man? What problems did he have? How did he die? What was his legacy? Was he brigand or prince? Farmer or merchant? Beggar or holy man? Perhaps this coin has been held in the hand of all of those and more. Think about it."

J.B. turned the coin slightly so that the reflection traveled along the ceiling and down onto the wall.

"This coin enables time travel. It takes our minds back five hundred years or four hundred years or two hundred years, and we find ourselves in bazaars or palaces or maybe in the tent of a desert brigand. We seek to know, our mind's eye inquiring. Our imaginations are fueled by the extrapolation of our knowledge. We are there. But to come home, we simply put the coin away." J.B. dropped the coin into his sweater pocket, and the reflection stopped traveling down the wall.

"It's that simple, Uncle Louis. It's great to go into the past, but we have to have a way home. This coin does that."

Louis, a wistful, almost enigmatic smile on his face, took J.B.'s hand. "I know you think you understand, but I don't think it's quite that simple. I wish it were."

"Oh, but it is," J.B. countered. "Dad told me about the recommendations for the Silver Stars. It seems that in both cases, lots of people you liked or knew died, even though you tried to save them. The citation says that you were cut off behind enemy lines and suffered from cerebral malaria. That you were wounded by shellfire but continued to lead your troops. You were wounded again on Iwo Jima and suffered a relapse of the malaria after stopping a Japanese counterattack.

"Uncle Louis, I'm only thirteen, and I wish I understood better, but I know it doesn't do any good being mad at God. Besides I don't think it's God you're mad at. Like Larry and Sophia in *The Razor's Edge*, you think it's wrong that somebody else died and you didn't. On the one hand, you feel guilty; on the other, you feel cheated—but neither is right.

"There may not be anything you can do about the relapse spells, but I think that if you want to come back sooner, you can. Just keep the coin in your pocket, and know that you can come back anytime you choose."

J.B. stood up, leaned over, and hugged his uncle, then headed upstairs to his bedroom.

H.B., who had been listening at the French doors into the dining room, entered quietly and sat next to his younger brother. Louis had tears in his eyes. H.B. put his arm around him and pulled him over so that Louis's head was on his shoulder.

Upstairs J.B. sat at his desk. He took his notebook out and began to write.

Why War Isn't the Answer

A twenty-year-old left his home in the beautiful port city of Mobile to defend his country in a war the country didn't want and tried to avoid. A twenty-year-old with exceptional musical talent, with the potential of youth, and with the future in his eyes…

It was a good Christmas.

THE UNOPENED GIFT

"WHAT SHALL I DO WITH this?" he asks, taking the small wrapped box from the mantel and blowing no more than a day's collection of dust from the top.

"Oh, we have to keep that," she answers, looking up briefly from the cardboard box into which she is carefully packing small, bubble-wrapped, porcelain figurines.

"What's in it?" He turns the small box in his hands, admiring the multicolor butterflies that adorn the white paper. Butterflies of yellow and orange, blue and purple—the paper is folded with the most symmetric of corners and held in place around the four-inch cube with a Tiffany blue ribbon tied in the most perfect of bows.

"Don't know," she answers.

"You don't know?" His voice conveys incredulity.

"Nope. Never have."

"Shouldn't we open it then and find out?" His curiosity is peaked.

"Nope, not going to open it."

"Well then, does anybody know what's in it?"

"Only my great-grandfather, and he's been dead for thirty years."

"OK, let me understand this. Your great-grandfather knew what was in here, but no one else does?" He is a little frustrated.

"That's correct." She enjoys making him work for the information.

"So then, why hasn't somebody opened the box to find out? Maybe it's something valuable. A family heirloom? A watch, maybe? Or maybe a brooch or..."

He pauses to think, then goes on. "Well, it could be most anything that could fit into this box. Maybe it's a diamond or emerald ring. Or maybe a diamond AND emerald ring!" He imagines the great wealth such a box could hold.

"Yes," she answers. "It could be any of those things. But it probably isn't."

"But I thought you said you didn't know what's in here." He thrusts the box in her direction to emphasize his predicament.

"No, but I know the story. Before I share it, though...first, look closer at the paper, and tell me what you see."

He pulls the box back toward himself and, holding it in two hands, begins to turn it around, looking closely at each of the six sides. "Well, it's a good quality paper." He runs his finger along one of the crisp creases in the folds of the box. "It's not all shiny and thin like most wrapping paper."

"That's because it isn't wrapping paper," she instructs him. "It's a very fine-quality stationer's paper. Now look closer at the butterflies."

He steps to the window so that the morning sunshine, slanting through as it does in the cold days of January, illuminates the box.

"Why, they're drawn on, not printed!" He is surprised. There is an intricacy to the butterflies that did not show under the small, incandescent table lamp. "They're beautiful." He turns the box over and over in his hands, closely examining each of the exquisitely drawn butterflies.

"See," she says. "Now, look at how the paper is folded. See how each corner is near perfect? How the folds are practically faultless forty-five–degree angles?"

He does look and finds each corner as she says, a perfect fold splitting the ninety-degree corners in half. He thinks how shabby and coarse his wrapping usually looks when finished and admires the absolute perfectness of this small box.

"Now, the bow," she instructs. "Look at the symmetry of the bow."

Again, she is correct. The bow is perfectly proportional with loops of equal size and shape. "Yes, I see what you mean. I've never seen a gift wrapped so perfectly or with such artistic paper."

"There's more." She stands from her kneeling and folds herself backward onto the small sofa—hugging her knees to her chest in just the slightest protest to the coolness of the room.

"You see, that was my great-grandfather's Christmas gift to my great-grandmother the first year they were married. They had only been married for two months. Now, Great-Grandmother was almost a zealot when it came to symmetry and order, and she was no slouch at admiring beautiful things. Why, these Meissen porcelains are hers as well, but they're from much later in her married life. Well, anyway, so this was very early in their marriage; they were just starting out. They didn't have much in the way of money, so I doubt there's a diamond ring or gold bracelet in the box; but my great-grandmother was so taken with the paper, the art, and the symmetry that she refused to undo it to discover what was underneath. She said that while it remained wrapped, it represented a perfectness in its beauty and symmetry, and that she could imagine whatever she wanted was contained within. And she did. Then my grandmother after her, my mother, and now it's my turn."

She puts out her hand and gently takes the gift from him. There is a slight weight to the box; it isn't empty. She holds it in front of her, admiring once again the symmetry of the folds, the skillfulness of her great-grandfather's inked drawings, the perfectness of the Tiffany blue bow.

"Still," he says in a voice ever so slightly vexed. "I wonder what's in it."

She fixes him with crystal-blue eyes. "Oh, you already know the answer if you listened to the story."

"I do?" He loves her, but sometimes she can be extremely obtuse.

"Of course you do. This box contains the gift of hope. It's the perfect Christmas gift."

She smiles at him.

ABOUT THE AUTHOR

TONY JORDAN GREW UP IN Mobile, Alabama, and graduated cum laude from the University of the South in Sewanee, Tennessee—where he studied religion and theology. He served as a combat rescue and special operations helicopter pilot in Southeast Asia and later as an instructor, test pilot, and squadron commander in the US Air Force.

In 1978, he was recruited into the Central Intelligence Agency and became a clandestine operations officer. During his almost twenty-seven-year career with the CIA, he was awarded many of the CIA's highest commendations for achievement. After seven field assignments as an undercover operative and numerous senior leadership positions, he retired to accept a vice presidency with a Boston-based research and technology firm.

In 2015, he began writing novels and short stories in the tower office of his cottage on Spy Hill Farm, in the foothills of the Crab Orchard Mountains of Tennessee. He is ably supported and appropriately encouraged, when needed, by his wife, Anne, and his BFF, Tailwagger Jack.

If you enjoyed this book, please consider writing and posting a review online. Reviews on Amazon and Goodreads are particularly appreciated. Independent authors live on word of mouth and exposure through sites like these, so anything you can do to help publicize this and other books will help tremendously.

www.ingramcontent.com/pod-product-compliance
Lightning Source LLC
Chambersburg PA
CBHW070338130626
46556CB00007B/2920